"Beneath the impeccable surface of Navarro's ice-cold prose, dread and grief wrestle in a territory of uncanny shadows. Like the work of many great fantasists before her—Robert Walser, Leonora Carrington, Witold Gombrowicz, Remedios Varo—Navarro takes alien landscapes and turns them into eerily apt mirrors of our most secret realities. Grimly comedic, deeply affecting, these stories are a necessary poison, one that revives instead of destroys, emboldens rather than deadens. In spite of all the ghosts, madnesses, nightmares, and grotesque transformations they are subject to, her characters manage to make their own maps, turning endings into beginnings, disgust into love, death to peace: *Rabbit Island* is a series of unforgettable journeys designed by a master cartographer."

—MARYSE MEIJER, author of
The Seventh Mansion and *Rag: Stories*

"On the farthest edges of radical honesty, Navarro discovers something surreal. Reading *Rabbit Island* is like spending a week at an abandoned hotel with rooms inhabited by haunted bunnies and levitating grandmothers. Dark, brilliant, and addictive."

—SANDRA NEWMAN, author of *The Heavens*

"The stories in *Rabbit Island* are as surprising and delightful as they come. Here there are no mundane worlds: wherever an Elvira Navarro story begins, it eventually leads to the uncanny borderlands between dream and nightmare, love and fear, science and mystery, all of which are, of course, reality itself."

—MATT BELL, author of *Appleseed*

RABBIT ISLAND

Also by Elvira Navarro from Two Lines Press

A WORKING WOMAN

RABBIT ISLAND

STORIES

Elvira Navarro

Translated from Spanish by Christina MacSweeney

TWO LINES
PRESS

Originally published in Spanish as: *La isla de los conejos*
Published in coordination with
Casanovas & Lynch Literary Agency, S. L.
Copyright © 2019 by Elvira Navarro

English Translation © 2020 by Christina MacSweeney

Two Lines Press
582 Market Street, Suite 700, San Francisco, CA 94104
www.twolinespress.com

ISBN: 978-1-949641-09-7
Ebook ISBN: 978-1-949641-10-3

Library of Congress Cataloging-in-Publication Data:
Names: Navarro, Elvira, 1978– author. | MacSweeney, Christina, translator.
Title: Rabbit island / Elvira Navarro; translated from the Spanish by
Christina MacSweeney. Description: San Francisco, CA: Two Lines Press,
[2021] | Originally published in Spain as *La isla de los conejos* in 2019. |
Summary: "Eleven stories that traverse a gritty, surreal terrain between
madness and freedom" --Provided by publisher.
Identifiers: LCCN 2020024001 (print) | LCCN 2020024002 (ebook) |
ISBN 9781949641097 (trade paperback) | ISBN 9781949641103 (ebook)
Classification: LCC PQ6714.A827 A2 2021 (print) | LCC PQ6714.A827
(ebook) | DDC 863/.7--dc23
LC record available at https://lccn.loc.gov/2020024001
LC ebook record available at https://lccn.loc.gov/2020024002

Cover design by Gabriele Wilson
Cover photo by Avigator Fortuner/Shutterstock.com
Design by Jessica Sevey
Printed in Canada

1 3 5 7 9 10 8 6 4 2

Support for the translation of this book was provided by Acción
Cultural Española, AC/E. This project is also supported in part by an
award from the National Endowment for the Arts.

CONTENTS

Gerardo's Letters   3

Strychnine   23

Rabbit Island   29

Regression   41

Paris Périphérie   55

Myotragus   61

Notes on the Architecture of Hell   73

The Top Floor Room   93

Memorial   115

Gums   133

The Fortune-Teller   155

GERARDO'S LETTERS

I'm on the bus listening to Stevie Wonder on my iPod. Gerardo's patience is wearing thin. There's a song that's you. To block out Gerardo, I use all my might to visualize you. Why am I here, on a journey I don't even want to be making? Where are you now? I've turned off my cellphone for fear that you'll call while he's here. He was annoyed when I showed up late, had even gone out of the bus station to see if I was coming so he could tell the driver that I was waiting for the light to cross the street. "I was ready to tell him to leave without you."

It's still raining. He's taken my hand. "I don't want us to argue on this trip." I have to take off my headphones and make him repeat what he's said, and that really bothers him, although I don't mind letting him suffer for my sins: he wants to trust me. Later, I'm ashamed of my pettiness, but I keep telling myself that he asks for it. Plus his hand feels heavy. It's weighing me down. I think about you, think that I've taken this journey out of cowardice, and the waves of rage wash over me again; I have to get free before his weight crushes me, shrug off his head resting on my shoulder. Brusquely, I push it away; I stand up and pretend to look for a book in my backpack.

There's some consolation. He really does believe I'm trying to find something. He got wet standing in the drizzle, he's shivering and looks so vulnerable and patient that I calm down. It's just two days. Two days and it'll be finished.

The hostel is about three kilometers from Talavera. We take a cab. There's no one at the front desk, but through an open door come the sounds of a television and the flickering light of the screen. I walk into the large lounge and say, "Hello?" A man, who's been dozing, sprawled on the couch, gets to his feet—I'm not tall, but he's shorter, though not quite achondroplastic. Without saying a word, without even a smile, he leads us back to the lobby. He has a flat, course-featured face. Greasy hair, grubby clothes—frayed jeans and a dark crimson sweater—big clumsy hands with dirty nails. "We have a reservation." "Gerardo de Paco?" "That's right." "Can I have your ID?" A cavernous, stealthy voice. Shorty heads for the stairs, holding the key to our room. We follow. Third floor. A white hallway with bare light bulbs hanging from the ceiling. He puts the key in the lock. The room is a good size, but doesn't even have a sink. Gerardo watches my face. He observes me, taking my revulsion for granted. That's how well he knows me. That well.

He's closed the door. This is what I know: I'm alone in a room with Gerardo, our luggage still packed, the night pulsing outside. Outside, beyond a tiny window covered with green mosquito netting, covered, closed.

"So?"

"A bit dirty," I say.

He bends over his backpack and extracts an old radio. Then he stands up and takes off his parka. The way he moves is a model of efficiency, a reproach. With a joint between his lips and the sports station playing at deafening volume, he lies back on one of the beds to demonstrate his ability to make himself at home anywhere. And just like when he bent over his backpack (it contains only the bare essentials, all of them perfectly organized; and then there's the backpack itself: not only cheap—he hates using brand names—but one of his best-ever buys, the weight well distributed between the shoulders and hips so he can walk comfortably while carrying it, and with just the right number of pockets, and straps for attaching up to three sleeping bags. It's nothing like mine, which isn't even a backpack, but a vaguely sporty bag bought in El Corte Inglés, and which in addition to being expensive is impractical, as useless as they come and so on), the way he lies on the bed with his buttocks and thighs on a grubby checked blanket covered in hairs is a condemnation of me, and I'm breathing, chewing, and smelling blanket full of hair and grime.

"Shall we have dinner?"

"We can ask if there's anything left," he replies, holding out the joint to me. I shake my head. "Just let me finish this."

"If we wait any longer they'll have closed the kitchen."

Unwillingly, he follows me to the large TV lounge.

I haven't been hungry for months. Since I told him, I've had no appetite for anything. Shorty is half asleep on the couch. This time it's Gerardo who speaks:

"Excuse me, can we get sandwiches or something?"

Shorty scrutinizes us from the shadows with an astonished expression, as if we were ghostly presences whose voices he can't hear.

"One moment," he says.

Soon afterward he returns and, with a grimace, beckons us into the equally spacious dining room adjoining the large lounge; at the far end is a gleaming metal counter for sliding the trays piled at its left-hand side. He points to a table and goes into the kitchen, coming back with a selection of dishes: lima beans in garlic, sausages, dried-out Spanish omelet. The table has a green checked cloth with tomato stains. The cutlery is dirty too. I start to eat. Shorty disappears.

"Not so bad, is it?"

I shrug. What I want to say is: "It's disgusting."

"What do you expect for ten euros?" Gerardo continues.

Back in the bedroom, I sit on a chair and look at him. He's serious. The bags under his eyes sag down over his cheekbones, he's lost seven kilos. He's taken the remains of the joint from the ashtray and is smoking it.

"You do your own thing. I'm going to take a look around," I say.

I open the door, glance back at the blank screen of my cellphone peeking out from my bag. Gerardo notices that glance, is aware of my suspicions. But anyway, I go out into the hall, which divides into two wings. One way leads to the staircase, two narrow passages with red doors splitting off. At the far end a young girl in a bathrobe is sitting on a stool. A boy comes out of a room and asks if she's done with the homework. "No," she replies. The bathrobe is open to her thighs, allowing a glimpse of gleaming, pearly legs. A third guy joins them and they talk about the math topics covered in the university entrance exam. They are seniors in high school, I think, staying in the hostel for the semester. Teenagers from the villages in the Sierra de Gredos. Their greedy eyes, fixed on me, make me feel uncomfortable and I turn away before the words clamoring to get out of their mouths can become spiderwebs. I walk back along the labyrinth of hallways and red doors and descend the stairs. The spacious TV lounge is empty and dark. I switch on a light: a horror vacui of celebrities covers one wall. There are large posters, but also postcards and magazine clippings. I recognize: Ava Gardner, Humphrey Bogart, Vivien Leigh, Marilyn Monroe, and Sara Montiel. The New Kids on the Block stand over the TV and, covering the window, Alejandro Sanz and the Spice Girls smile out at me.

"You love these places," comes Gerardo's voice from the back of the room, and it's only then that I perceive the smell of hash in the air and the putrid damp.

It's him, I think, but it could also have been Shorty, who is now crouched down between the faux leather couches, stalking some prey.

We go back to the bedroom, where my cellphone is also spying on me with its silence. I switch it on.

"Are you expecting a call?" asks Gerardo.

His voice is unsteady; he breathes as if he's suffocating.

"No."

"Why did you turn off your phone?"

"To save the battery."

"You told me that you'd broken up with him. That you don't even call each other now."

"Sorry," I mumble.

I grab my toothbrush and go to the bathroom, worrying about my phone, in spite of having erased the compromising messages. When I return, it's sitting where I left it, but I continue to feel anxious until Gerardo goes to the bathroom and I can check that there isn't, in fact, anything on it to give me away.

I sit on the bed—the grubby blanket covered in hairs—and wait. He reappears with a damp toiletry bag. His air of efficiency has vanished. He picks up my phone. Checks it compulsively. I watch the missed calls scroll past, the outgoing calls, the messages. I'm getting annoyed. He puts the phone on the nightstand and looks ashamed.

"You should change your password. Sorry."

"Don't apologize."

"Sorry," he repeats.

He lies down, puts on his headphones, and smokes. I undress and get between the sheets.

"Switch off the light," I say.

I calculate that it must be about two. I'm not sleepy. I try to work out a strategy for leaving him, for walking out on him in the morning, or maybe on Sunday, when we're back in Madrid, to say that it's over, that I've had enough, and that I only came on this trip to put an end to it all because there's no point going on…but I can't. Gerardo's angst is pasted onto my body, it immobilizes me.

A couple of years ago we had a six-month separation, when I accepted a job in Brussels, and while I was there I wrote him long letters (at that time I still believed that emails violated the principle of delay). He never commented on the things I told him. It was as if they had been replaced by something else, and the result of that something else couldn't just be called jealousy, even though that was the driving force behind it all: his jealousy, which used to flay me with some weird form of animus, as though I had to pay for future injuries. At first, I took no notice and continued writing to him. Then, as his listless voice on the telephone and his silence about my letters piled up, I began to feel guilty for writing. Those letters never mentioned anything that might arouse suspicion, but it seemed as though telling him about the walks I took was a cover for some grubby reality, on which he had the last word.

The silence in this room, in this hallway, in this hostel, is Gerardo's silence about my letters. It makes no difference what I say. There's only his obsession, and I meet every one of its expectations: I behave as if talking about hairs on blankets is a way of not mentioning something else. And although his mania is justified now, the result is the same as when I was living in Brussels and not cheating on him. What's really happening isn't particularly important, or is only important now because his fears have finally taken physical form. And how—lying here between the sheets with his desire prolonging the silence—can I avoid

9

sensing his disgusting attempts to make me open my mouth. There are many nights when I lie awake, waiting for him to go to sleep, for the sheer pleasure of not hearing him, the pleasure of his silence. Then I become aware of the muscles in my legs relaxing, resting lightly on the bed, my respiration slowing, and it seems like a miracle to be able to sleep and move and live as I please, without Gerardo watching me.

The day is gray. Or that's how it seems through the green mosquito netting. We go down to the front desk to ask how to get to Talavera and Shorty says that if we wait, he'll give us a lift. Ten minutes later he reappears in a new white Citroën C5. We climb in the back seat; it's freezing inside the car. Shorty doesn't close the doors. Gerardo eventually asks:

"Is someone else coming?"

"No," he replies.

He doesn't, however, move off; the doors of the C5 are still open.

"We'd like to get to Talavera quite soon. In time for breakfast."

"You could have gotten a coffee from the machine. Or woken up and shaken a leg earlier. Breakfast finishes at eleven here."

With three rapid movements, he closes the doors; Gerardo whispers, "What's with him? Is he stupid or something?" and I put a hand on his arm to calm him. I want to avoid an argument so that Shorty doesn't drive like a maniac, which I think will happen if he gets into a fight with Gerardo. Journeys along narrow back roads really disturb me, I become superstitious, and behind any raised voice I hear the screech of tires, collisions, see bodies flying through the air. It's so bad that whenever I get into a car I prepare to die. But Shorty drives slowly, and what ends up bothering me is his lack of urgency. All of a sudden, I want the C5 to accelerate and thus crystallize my fear, which is not fear now, but the thrill of letting myself be carried away by speed, the sensation of not giving a damn if we crash. In Talavera we eat sandwiches and visit the ceramics museum. Then we spend a few hours walking around the bitingly cold city, with its unalleviated back-alley ambience. We hitch a ride back to the hostel and, as the idea of going up to the bedroom scares me, I insist on taking a walk before nightfall. Two roads, separated by a wasteland approximately a kilometer wide, run parallel to the building. I suggest we cross them, but Gerardo says it's late, and we'd be better off exploring closer to home. I acquiesce, although I still have the urge to cross the limits of the landscape—this anxiety to know what lies beyond always makes me hurry, as if I'm late in arriving somewhere. We walk in a straight line until the darkness is absolute, and then turn back, guided by the lights from the hostel and the passing cars. We can't even see our sneakers, and keeping our eyes fixed on the ground makes us nervous, as though any minute we might fall face first or step into a scorpion's nest. More than walking, it feels like our feet are sinking into the earth like talons. When we get to the basketball courts, I ask Gerardo to brace my knees while

I do some abs. The cold ground makes it hard to bend; the sense of having Gerardo crouching near me, his head brushing my knees, becomes unpleasant and I stop. I feel absurd but think that getting wrapped up in each other's manias is what couples do. Things like that are part and parcel of the whole romantic rigmarole, of the idea that you find a special person who loves you, and whom you love, and who gives his blessing to all your personal eccentricities, like doing an ab workout at nine at night on a dark basketball court three kilometers from Talavera. Perhaps there's something good in all of it, something I've lost sight of; perhaps the absurdity only applies to moribund relationships, like mine and Gerardo's. He claims that everyone else accepts that rigmarole without question. "You're crazy," he tells me when I voice such arguments, and then I experience my craziness as a lacerating loneliness, even as true madness; I don't know if I'm crazy, or if it's Gerardo making me think I am. In his company, I lose my sanity, and given that Gerardo has usurped sound judgment, I assume that without him I'll be unable to find my way in the world.

In the dining room, the trays are being taken away. It isn't even ten; we ask an elderly lady wearing a hairnet why they close so early. She says that if we want to eat later we can go to a proper hotel. The menu: Spam with peas and perfectly elliptical schnitzels whose greasy coating conceals an agglomeration of minced chicken cuts. I only eat the peas. The Spam and the chicken are the same pale pink. "These schnitzels haven't been cooked through," comments Gerardo. At one of the tables the girl from the night before is chatting with seven boys; together they must compose the sum total of the students. They have finished their meal and are smoking, flicking the ash into a plastic cup; they then stub out their cigarettes in the remains of their food.

"I'm going to take a shower," I announce as we enter our bedroom.

I extract my bathrobe and slippers from my bag, and am already at the door when Gerardo says:

"You can get undressed here. I promise not to touch."

I turn my back and start to strip. I'm aware of his determination to be noticed; it's a disagreeable weight at the back of my neck that causes me to get tangled up in my jeans and fall over. I get back to my feet and walk out the door in my bathrobe, still wearing my bra and T-shirt. The showerhead spits water in fits and starts, but I stand under it until the skin on my fingers goes wrinkly and the bathroom mirror is misted. I pace up and down, opening the doors of the other shower cubicles, where those black bugs that inhabit dark, shady places are scuttling around. I slam the doors, frightening away the bugs; eventually, a whole colony is flying around the mirror, from which a swarm of droplets falls. My feet are cold, and I decide to get in the shower again; but a plague of insects is crawling up the walls of the cubicle and I don't have the courage to chase them out. I go back to the room. Gerardo is jacking off with his jeans around his knees. He doesn't look at me. I quickly grab my clothes and, with the cord of the hairdryer trailing behind, leave the room before he ejaculates.

I take refuge in the bathroom, where the insects are

now in the corners of the shower cubicles. I'm worried that there won't be an outlet; but if not, I can always go to the lounge and dry my hair there. I imagine the high school students sprawling on the faux leather couches watching *Big Brother 3*; I'm surprised that I can't visualize them watching any other program and—rationalizing this inability—I decide that it must have to do with my mood.

The thought of having to ask the students' permission to use the hairdryer while they are enjoying the show isn't appealing, but I'm determined not to return to the bedroom; this way Gerardo will think Shorty has cut my body up and put the pieces in the freezer by the swimming pool bar. It's a good moment for us to finish once and for all: I'll go back upstairs for my luggage at six in the morning, while he's still asleep, and then call a cab. For any other couple, that breaking-up plan might be unimaginable without the police searching the village for the absent partner; but Gerardo and I are used to behaving weirdly. If I felt like spending the day hanging from the branch of a tree, he wouldn't give it a second thought. That's another of the things that, almost a year ago, made it unthinkable to leave him: I detest conventionality. With him, by taking everything to extremes—rage to extremes, thinking to extremes, disgust to extremes—I achieve some form of exasperated life, and believe that the force of that exasperation will hurl me somewhere.

Fortunately, there's an electrical socket in the bathroom. As I've forgotten to bring my comb, I attempt to untangle my hair with my fingers, making the top layer and my bangs more or less presentable: the climate in Talavera isn't dry enough to stop my hair from frizzing, although it's likely that this has less to do with Talavera than the microclimate of the bathroom, the damp mist evaporating from the floor tiles, redolent of plumbing and swamps. My nascent dreadlocks fall in ringlets, like the coiffure of someone in a crinoline skirt, but what really annoys me is not having brought my eyelash curler or my green eyeliner so I might get at least one part of my face in shape, achieve some sort of beauty that will nudge me toward a kinder appraisal of myself. I leave the bathroom carrying the hairdryer and pass our door on tiptoe, heading for the stairs. Gerardo must have been listening for my footsteps because, when I get to the landing, he turns the lock and opens the door. I run and don't stop until I'm in the lobby. I'm euphoric.

"Natalia?" he calls from two floors above.

I don't answer.

"Natalia? Is that you?" he repeats, and my euphoria dissolves into pity.

I start walking, not worrying about making noise, or that he might come down and see me going outside again.

The TV lounge is empty. It's Saturday. Why had it never occurred to me that the high school students would have gone to Talavera? I wonder if they walk down, taking it for granted that they don't have cars, that their only transportation is the bicycles on which they do balancing acts along the ditch in the nonexistent moonlight. In one corner of the room a router connected to a computer is blinking, and my fingers itch to open my email. I have the sense that, having not checked my account for the entire day, some critical piece of news must be waiting for me. I also harbor the vague hope that there might be a message from you. The computer takes ages to boot up, and the room is so cold that I plug in the hairdryer and place it next to the keyboard, cursing Gerardo, but at the same time enjoying the sensation of being pissed off at him again because even an ounce of pity would jeopardize my resolve.

There are four unimportant emails in my inbox. I answer them mechanically, then drag one of the couches over and plug the hairdryer into the adaptor by the TV so I can watch it with a stream of warm air blowing on my legs. It's so cold that my breath seems to be freezing in the air. I tell myself that it must be warmer outdoors, that it's only icy inside the hostel. The posters of singers covering the window prevent me from seeing just how long the building is, and I'm tempted to go outside to check. I could take a stroll to the basketball courts; if I had my coat, I could even sit and gaze at the stars. I need to do something; here, curled up on the faux leather, with the hairdryer resting on the instep of my left foot, I'm not sure if I'll be able to hold out until morning. However, leaving my refuge would mean meeting Gerardo, because he's now the one walking up and down the hallways, the one who's gone out to smoke a joint on the grass and throw a stone into the scummy water. I sit watching a documentary about trans fats and, when it's over, leave the room, with the impression that the temperature has risen slightly.

A shopping-mall-white light is coming from the swimming pool bar, and I'm certain that Gerardo must be there with Shorty. That light erases any sense of intimacy, and as I cross the threshold it occurs to me that I'm going to be subjected to an interrogation. I'm dressed, but it's as if I were naked. I have the feeling that my thoughts and what I've been doing in the TV lounge are on view, but I don't have the energy to leave the bar. Four of the high school students are sitting at a table with bottles of beer before them. Gerardo and Shorty are drinking together; Gerardo is smoking a joint; he's frowning, deep in conversation. But even so, he can't help but say:

"The TV doesn't belong to you. These kids probably wanted to watch a movie."

The students make no response. Their eyes are red; I guess Gerardo has passed a few joints around. The noise of the hairdryer has isolated me from the nightlife of the hostel; it's not so different from the dives Gerardo and I frequent: a strange place where you can learn something or have a unique—usually synonymous with sordid—experience. A place that fits our tendency to take everything to the limit. But I need a few beers to wind down and settle, with no sense of guilt, into our usual routine—just for this one last night, and then it's over. I ask Shorty for a Mahou; he points to the fridge. I can't find the bottle opener, but say nothing; I rummage around on the counter, which is piled with glasses, cups, and teaspoons. Gerardo hands me the opener.

"Thanks," I say.

He doesn't reply. He's nodding at whatever Shorty is

saying. I stand behind the counter until I've finished my beer and then take another from the fridge; then I come out, at a loss for what to do next. The bar has two doors: one leads to the lobby; the other is an exit. I don't know if that one is open, but there's a key in the lock. I walk over and give it a gentle tweek, trying not to attract attention. My delicacy achieves nothing, and I swing from side to side in an attempt to turn the key, which leaves its imprint on my skin. In the hushed bar (the high school students are either talking in whispers or not saying anything), where Gerardo and Shorty are like a pair of actors on stage, my gyrations must resemble the behavior of a woman who works in a very cheap restaurant on Calle Atocha: she insults the customers as she serves their meals, swearing loudly, as if she were singing. Her song and the clicking of her heels interrupt the murmurs of the diners, who sometimes laugh quietly, but mostly view the poor woman's lack of restraint with grave expressions, while she alternates between normal conversations and foul language, managing not to offend anyone, or maybe not even having to try since the voice she uses for swearing is different from her conversational one, as if she had a devil in her throat. I succeed in opening the door and go outside, certain that I won't have the courage to reenter the bar. I down my beer at an incredible rate to achieve a pleasant state of alcohol-induced passivity as quickly as possible, so that I won't feel self-conscious walking past Gerardo and Shorty, not to mention the high school students, because by now there's no escaping my tendency to humiliate myself just to be accepted. It could also be that my compulsive drinking and belief that I'll feel completely at ease once I'm inebriated are a cover for my desire to submit to Gerardo and, through him, enter the real world. I've noticed the looks Shorty gives me for not staying close to my boyfriend, for not living up to his expectations of the behavior of the partner of this man he's getting along well with and who is playing up to him so amazingly. I sit on the steps and watch the occasional truck pass; this isn't a swimming pool bar, as I'd initially thought, but some sort of roadhouse, even if it doesn't function as such; maybe it's just a game room for the students.

Feeling the effects of the first two beers, I go inside for a third. I walk on air to the counter; the opener is in my possession, although that's not really important since Gerardo, Shorty, and the students have moved on to gin and tonics. A mild hubbub—the students are suddenly speaking more loudly, interrupting one another—has eased the atmosphere, and I lean against the pool table. I've left the door ajar, and the cold air enters, stirring the smoke from the joints and cigarettes, making it rise to the ceiling and momentarily form small clumps of cloud. Shorty watches me; his disapproval has morphed into a repulsive desire that must be directed at the girl who is studying in Talavera, that Scarlet Johansson of La Mancha. It pains me that her cheerful, animal innocence should be confronted with Shorty's lust. I scowl in disgust; he sees and passes a finger across his lips and blows me a quick, pathetic kiss. A sick, senseless gesture. Gerardo sees the gesture and pauses. Turning his back on his companion would mean losing a devotee, but he has passed the point where he can sit next to Shorty without becoming violent. Shorty is drunk enough not to notice the change in Gerardo's mood. Gerardo, for his part, is ready to ditch him, although what he's really hoping for is an argument with me. I stand up and grab four beers to see us through. Then I say to Shorty:

"Put them on our bill."

He mutters some obscenity, points at me, and laughs. We leave the bar without saying goodnight.

Back in the room I sink my comb into the knots in my hair. It takes me quite a while to untangle them; while I'm doing this, Gerardo opens a Mahou, finishes his joint, and goes to the bathroom to brush his teeth. When he returns I'm curling my eyelashes. He doesn't speak; in fact, he seems to understand that my belated attempts to look presentable are because I'm leaving, and as I too now understand that fact—at first I don't know why I'm making such a big deal of combing out the knots in my hair, curling my eyelashes, and putting on eyeliner to make my reflection in the mirror appealing—our mood turns somber. It's five in the morning; I ask him to come down to the front desk with me because I'm afraid of Shorty. I call a cab. The bar is empty and smells of the pot Gerardo shared with the students. The cab takes half an hour to arrive; it's a white vehicle, similar to Shorty's, with the regulation interior light. The driver looks at us as though some member of our family has been stabbed and he's taking us to identify the body. When he realizes that Gerardo is staying, as we're wishing each other all the best, the driver looks less concerned, and I begin to love his serenity; he suddenly seems so sane to me, full of life, and I'm so happy that these attributes are going to accompany me on the journey to the train station, during this night—almost as dark as the last one—when the only things to see are the markings along the highway.

STRYCHNINE

1

She compares the ferry to a spacecraft, and thinks that the windows are similar to the compound eyes of certain insects. Then she sees the as-yet nameless character walking along the deck, saying just that. The character is a woman, and she exudes an air of measured, rational, calming coldness. She's speculating on what she observes, which is also cold: dirty, white material; a slight odor of damp earth, sweat, french fries, and fish.

It's going to be a third person narrative, as though she were a stranger to herself. She wants to enter this aura of serene iciness she has just imagined, which is also the tone she wants for her text. That seems the best way to try out her new brain, to anticipate what's going to happen.

But feeling a little pessimistic, she seeks conversation.

As she approaches an elderly couple, she doesn't attempt to control the trembling of her lower lip. She suspects they have noticed the paw hanging from her ear-lobe. Then she goes to the café. Beside her is a very pale, potbellied man of around forty, and she feels the urge to tell him everything. She ties back her hair into a pony-tail and glances between the bottles behind the counter at the mirror: her left ear is higher than the right. The man doesn't notice, even though the difference is obvious. The ear feels heavy, and it's been getting increasingly red over the last few hours.

2

She remembers that she visited the city of T a year ear-lier. The guide showed them around the cathedral and they went to the seafront. The light was soft, filtering through the mist. It must have been early afternoon, and although spring had hardly shown its face yet, it felt as though there were a scorching hot summer to come.

The guide led them to the southern end of the city wall, by the beach. She noted some foreign tourists walk-ing into the sea, still taking swigs from their cans of beer. Others had climbed onto the rocks of the breakwater that formed a path to a small island with an ochre fortress; the horizontal structure looked like a heap of earth floating on the ocean. But what she saw wasn't a military installa-tion or a clod of earth, but an excrescence sprouting from the city.

3

Finally, she disembarks. Rain has been falling through the whole crossing. It takes her an hour to get through customs; the cabs are mostly old Mercedes that smell of musty leather. She walks through the medina quarter, up the narrow streets that remind her of canyons. She's booked a room in a hotel that had its heyday more than a century before. It feels as though night is about fall, because angry gray clouds are crowding the sky, but in fact it's only three in the afternoon.

She crosses a terrace overlooking the bay. The desk clerk stares at her ear, and when he speaks there's mockery in his voice.

The hotel is in shadows. Her room has two beds, shabby blankets, wall hangings that look like they've been hanging on the walls since 1870, when the hotel was built. Only the bathroom is new.

She attempts to write her story but gets no further than making a few scant notes. She numbers them. When the storm has passed, she leaves the hotel and goes into the souq, where she sees groups of women. Shopkeepers are offering them chickens, beans, onions. The carcasses of lambs, slashed from sternum to pelvis, spread the sour smell of blood over the dirty, greasy sidewalk, littered with disgarded vegetable leaves and offal.

She reaches the area where fabrics and argan oil are sold and decides to buy a hijab. In one of the stores she enters, countertop figures without breasts or facial features dominate the otherwise plain interior: half-finished mannequins wearing colorful headscarves.

She wants a black hijab. "You're married to a Muslim," says the man. It's a statement not a question. "I'm a Berber," he adds. She doesn't answer, just tries to put on the hijab standing in front of the Berber, who by now has noticed her ear. The man jokes with a soap vendor across the street; she can't work out how to wear the hijab and leaves the store without haggling over the price.

Back in the hotel, she mulls over how to fictionalize what has happened. She wants to leave an explanation, a trace of her process. But why? Aren't the words themselves enough? She finds it difficult to hold her pencil, as if, instead of her hand, it's the paw hanging from her ear that is attempting to write. It's all happening too quickly.

That night, looking out over the bay, she's surprised at how unmoved she is by the sight of the distant lights on the other shore, crystal clear after the fury of the storm. She feels nothing, not even the fear that might be expected given the uncertainty of the coming days or months. She has no idea how long her transformation will last. But what most astonishes her is that, even when she thinks about the people closest to her, it's as though they belong in the memory of another person.

4

She wakes at eleven the following morning and notes that her ear feels heavy and painful; when she moves, she hears a squeaking noise. Repulsion is immediately displaced by the absolute precision of the things around her, which seem shinier than before and have a coarse, mobile texture that made her think they were covered in a layer of multicolored insects. The chair smells different from the tapestries on the wall. She identifies: dust, cat hair, ebony, tamarisk, dandruff, opium, and strychnine.

The paw is now hanging below her breast. It's larger than the span of a hand now and has sprouted toes with small mouths. The toes flex like spiders' legs. When she sits at the desk, before her scant, numbered notes, the toes pick up her pen. The extremity squeaks; it's covered in a viscous varnish. She doesn't dare touch it. Her earlobe is red; blood is accumulating in the capillaries. She watches her new extremity move toward the scribbled writing on one side of her notes, a ballpoint pen between its toes. It adds to the scribbles. She attempts to make out what it's writing with so much concentration and at such a furious pace, but when she tugs away the pen, the paw tugs back. It resists even more strongly when she ties it to her hair with elastic bands. The moaning of the toes changes to frantic mutterings and the extremity kicks out rather unconvincingly at her shoulder. Then it calms and she feels its relaxation spilling down her side. What would happen if she cut it off?

She checks her cellphone. Why not call her mother and tell her what is happening? What use are these incomprehensible, numbered notes? She imagines a now huge paw creeping to the post office and putting them in an envelope. And her mother, dark circles under her eyes, trying to read those notes, doubly unintelligible due to the additional scrawls of the paw.

She goes back to the desk. The flowers and geometrical motifs of the hangings covering the walls are hypnotic. They seem to move, although in fact it's mites crawling through the threads of the old, moth-eaten fabric. She hears that mute army, distinguishes the nuances of its movements. The mites jump, stop, scuttle through the fine strands like tiny rats, like fleas through long hair. Seventy, eighty, a hundred years of dust has accumulated in those hangings, which to her eyes don't look faded now. There are also microscopic particles that were once desert sand. Something so old that it can no longer be named pulses within the weaves.

The next day the paw is ten centimeters longer. Since it's impossible to tie it back, she decides to return to the headscarf store. Outside, the world radiates light. The paw swings back and forth, as if it too is enjoying the bright, cheerful morning, and passersby stare at the bulge wrapped in something that is neither Western nor Arab clothing.

"I'd like three hijabs," she says in bad French.

The mannequins are more real than the vendor. She doesn't hide the paw from him; his face pales as he watches it timidly reaching out its three toes toward him. He runs screaming out of the store. She races after him; her intention is not to frighten him, but to pay for the hijabs, although halfway into her flight she forgets the reason for the pursuit. All of a sudden the man seems like her prey. He's thin, like a greyhound. But she can run faster.

RABBIT ISLAND

He'd built a canoe and wanted to try it out on the Guadalquivir River. Sports didn't interest him, and he hadn't made the canoe for regular use; once he'd explored the small river islands, it would be relegated to the junk room or sold. He thought of himself as an inventor, although the things he made couldn't be called inventions. Yet he'd begun to categorize all the ideas he sketched out in that way because he never used instruction manuals. His method was to work out for himself what was needed to construct something that had already been made. The process took months, and he considered it his true vocation: inventing things that had already been invented. The pleasure he got from that activity was something like what Sunday hikers feel when they reach the summit of some mountain and wonder why personal fulfillment is such a strange sensation. In the mornings the non-inventor taught in an arts and crafts college without any sense of fulfillment, despite the fact that his students found his workshops useful.

Since childhood he'd had the desire to travel to spits of land that extended into the sea, or to uninhabited islands. Once, when he was eighteen, his mother and father invited him to go with them to Tabarca, promising that it was a deserted island. He'd thought that it would be a wilderness, but what he found was seven streets of poor houses, a high wall, a church, a lighthouse, two hotels, and a small harbor. His parents had probably exaggerated the isolation of Tabarca to persuade him to spend the vacation with them—they didn't like the idea of leaving him home alone; but it's also possible they had never really understood what he meant by uninhabited places.

It was no easy task to count the number of river islands on the stretch of the Guadalquivir that adjoined the city. Some could be mistaken for small isthmuses. One September morning he walked to the dock carrying his canoe and took to the water. He spent several days getting the hang of his vessel, but once he had, he started to explore. There had been no rain for weeks. The river was very low; the water was still and smelled really bad. He skirted the islands with a mixture of anxiety and astonishment, without ever managing to take the canoe ashore. He wasn't confident in his ability to make rapid maneuvers, feared that the shorelines might be muddy, that he would slip and his canoe would drift away. And the thought of having to swim back with his mouth tightly closed to avoid swallowing the putrid water scared him, as did the lush, brightly colored vegetation buzzing with insects and the layer of bird shit on the ground. A landscape he'd believed to be beautiful was no more than trees deformed by the weight of birds—or perhaps some disease—colonies of bugs, and shrubs rotted by the filth.

On his fifth day out in the canoe, he decided to explore beyond the bend in the Guadalquivir. Paddling south had the advantage of allowing him to keep the low rolling hills of the surrounding countryside in sight. The islets there were tiny, more rocky, and packed close together like a rash. He paddled laboriously around them; near the last one he found a dead body floating facedown in the reeds. It was a man, wearing only boxers; the skin on his back was covered in blisters the size of a hand. He didn't know if they were caused by exposure to the sun, which was still scorching in September, or immersion in the water. The river stank. He called the civil defense unit and some officers arrived in a boat too big to pass through the reeds. They had a canoe onboard; while an obese officer was getting into it, he paddled over to the boat and asked for permission to leave. He didn't want to witness that dead flesh being dragged out of the water. He shrank at the thought of turning around to see fresh entrails being nibbled by fish.

The episode with the dead body kept him off the river for several days. When he recommenced his evening tours and, one day, found the courage to land on the island nearest the bank, he decided to inhabit it. He told himself that he'd had enough of urban life; the notion of doing something out of the ordinary was exciting. Those were just two of the harebrained ideas that sometimes accompanied him on his walks through the streets of his hometown, which seemed too self-obsessed, a spiral dragging him against his will to its core. But to be honest, he couldn't identify any underlying reason for his decision to occupy that narrow, nauseating stretch of land that would surely make him feel even worse than he did in the city.

Although it was the closest island to the riverbank, thick vegetation obscured the interior. He made a clearing in the center, cut down trees whose slender trunks looked more like lengths of rope. How did that spindly wood support so many branches, heavy with leaves? He decided to pitch a red tent instead of the usual khaki variety. The tent had good seals, but he was still panicked by the idea of waking up covered in insects. Maybe if he were to sleep higher up, he'd be safe from the maggots that blundered blindly along over the ground they desecrated, yet seemed able to sense their predators. The birds had no trouble catching them: they rootled in the sand with their beaks for that inexhaustible food supply. Perhaps, because those maggots were mostly water, and so insufficiently nutritious, the birds needed to hunt for more sophisticated insects to provide a richer diet. On a certain afternoon he examined one of the maggots. He placed it on his palm, where it reared up and danced. When he squeezed it lightly, it exploded like a tiny balloon.

He didn't sleep on the islet every night: that would have driven him crazy. It was enough to wake up there twice a week. When he did stay overnight on that tiny spot on the Guadalquivir, he'd hear only quiet murmers in the early hours. Except when the owls attacked, the birds were silent at night and the only sound was the occasional flapping of wings. They were tightly packed on the branches of the poplar trees, shielding their heads under their wings and puffing up their breasts, so the birds on the end would more often than not fall off. The noise that really bothered him wasn't those nocturnal descents but the squawking of the birds at sunset as they vied for roosts in the trees; it was loud enough to make any calculation of how many of them had alighted on that wretched piece of land impossible. There seemed to be thousands. For an hour their squawking would drill into his ears, and not even putting on headphones and playing music at top volume could drown it out. He even tried leaving his tent and shouting to try to scare them away, but the flock took no notice. His cries made as much impression on them as a scrap of seaweed in the middle of the ocean; or the birds perhaps mistook him for some weird member of their own kingdom. Even though he'd end up with strained vocal cords, he was loath to admit to himself that there was something cathartic about screaming and making grotesque gestures. He often lost any sense of time and would continue raging into the night, after the birds had already settled down; on these occasions, any of the few people who strolled along the riverbank would have looked across to the island, believing that the sounds came from some animal.

The birds came to the river island to sleep, breed, and die. The whole place was full of nests and excrement, and when the non-inventor returned home not even a shower got rid of the smell. Apparently those white birds were pests. That's what an old man who fished from the pier said. He asked what they were called but the man had no idea. The non-inventor tried searching the internet and found nothing there either. He flipped through a guide to the fauna of the Guadalquivir; the birds on the island didn't look like any of the egrets it described. That was as far as his research went; when you got down to it, discovering what species they were wouldn't change his resolve to become, one or two days a week, a human who bellowed at creatures that took no notice of him, that slept through the hail of stones he hurled at them. They didn't even deign to look at him when, in his rage, he shook the spindly trunks of the poplars. The treetops would sway violently; the rocking branches gave the impression of sturdy Andalusian festival-float bearers carrying the island on their shoulders.

As the weeks passed, he became convinced that his occupation of the island was legal. Why should he have to ask permission to inhabit a place that was empty? He found it impossible to believe that the other islands were untouched by human hands, but for him that wasn't the worst thing; what he couldn't bear was the lack of curiosity of the residents of a city with a population of over three hundred thousand. Was he the only one among so many people to visit what was right under their noses?

He started to leave money in his tent to see if anyone stole it. While the people whose work involved paddling canoes along the Guadalquivir weren't necessarily thieves, there must be crooks on the lookout for a windfall, or hungry vagrants who would surely pocket a large-denomination bill. He checked on a daily basis, but the fifty euros remained in place. The bill never moved. No one ever took the money. No one else set foot on the island.

When he wasn't inventing things that had already

been invented, the non-inventor made installations that he didn't call art. For instance, he'd removed the plush skins of ten toy dogs whose front legs moved and eyes lit up when they barked. Then he placed the skin under the dogs' paws and put the whole thing in a rabbit hutch. He devised a mechanism for remotely setting the de-plushed canines in motion. When friends came over, he'd press a button on the remote. Ten skinned toy dogs would bark and move their legs back and forth on their own hides, their yellow eyes aglow.

But when those friends suggested that he should sell the installation to some campaign for the protection of animals he just shrugged. Hadn't the idea already been used? At heart, he thought that if it had occurred to him, he must have already seen it somewhere. And so he refused to allow anyone to consider his installations art. He was terrified by the thought of having an exhibition and people commenting that his works were just copies of someone else's work. He wasn't sure why he was so frightened of that particular critique when he didn't actually believe in the concept of originality and often argued the point at great length, even if he were incapable of remembering the origins of his appropriations. Some other of his non-art pieces were: a mechanical flea circus inside a closet; a sandwich toaster made from two irons that he used to melt queso añejo into his guests' hands when he had a party; a pile of books with twenty years of accumulated dust whose importance lay in the fact that the dust—by then dirtballs—contained the dead cells of his deceased relatives.

It was the hutch with its de-plushed dogs that gave

him the idea of introducing rabbits onto the island to scare off the birds. He resolved not to stay overnight again: he was done with shouting. The tent could be left so he could observe the rabbits and take a nap. It was late fall, the clocks had gone back an hour, so it was no longer a wild idea to paddle to the island at four in the afternoon and enjoy the cool river air, although the water still stank as badly as it had in summer due to dry weather. He bought twenty rabbits—ten bucks and ten does—and they very quickly began to reproduce. Soon there wouldn't be enough food for them on the island. The non-inventor had calculated that the new inhabitants would attack the nests at ground level when they had nothing else to eat. If the birds could no longer breed on the island, they would go to another one.

The rabbits were pure white, with long fur and red eyes. They had been more expensive than the gray or brown ones, but he deemed it important that they were the same color as the birds. He told himself that using them to populate the island was his way of continuing to inhabit it. Eventually he even allowed them into the tent, which they seemed to like, no doubt because, since the ground wasn't suitable for constructing warrens, it provided protection from the sun. Inside the tent they gave birth to hairless little bunnies that resembled rats.

Once the rabbits had devoured the vegetation, nests began to be emptied of their eggs, a delicacy they seemed particularly fond of. On more than one occasion he witnessed them fight for the right to nibble the fine bluish shells. They didn't, however, argue over the chicks, and it was clear to the non-inventor that eating the warm flesh was something the rabbits did from necessity, reluctantly, as though their little minds rejected that cruelty. Their attitude, he thought, was in accord with the humanity they represented: his, their owner's, humanity. This is perhaps why he was surprised that, once their initial scruples were overcome, they didn't even leave the bones, as any person would have. They attacked the birds' throats with their sharp incisors, and a rim of blood the same color as their eyes would stain their wriggling noses and fine whiskers. Once they had eaten the meager flesh they would gnaw the skeleton clean; the sound was like the snapping of dry branches. They even ate the beak. Then they groomed themselves until their fur was white once again.

While the feast was in progress, the birds would fly overhead emitting anguished squawks. They hung around the scene of the crime for hours, as if their offspring might reappear from behind a stone. The non-inventor found it curious that they never thought to attack the rabbits. It would have been easy for them to peck out their eyes with their sharp beaks, but that sort of group behavior didn't seem to be instinctive to them.

It didn't enter into his calculations that the rabbits now being born on the island would only ever eat flesh and eggs, or that such an unnatural situation would have dire consequences. For a time, either from laziness or stupidity, the birds continued breeding on the island, but as the nests started to vanish the non-inventor realized that the litters of baby rabbits did too. One morning he witnessed the reason for this: they were being eaten by members of their own species. He found the spectacle horrific and renounced the idea that these animals were an extension of himself. In fact, he thought of them as pests, just like the birds, and if he continued going to visit them, it was simply because he felt guilty about abandoning creatures that he himself had debased.

One day he tried giving them rabbit food. They just sniffed it before returning to their somewhat gruesome sexual encounters. They had learned to reproduce in order to eat and, as a result, the frequency of mating had increased. The non-inventor realized that necessity had shortened the length of gestation. Everyone ate whenever a female produced young; while the silent birth was taking place, the rabbits observed the mother as if they were also considering eating her. And since the rabbits no longer showed any interest in the nests, the birds returned to breed.

The tent was visible from the riverbank, but that didn't bother him. His piece of land wasn't so different from camps set up by travelers or beggars under the bridges of the city's beltway, and as long as they didn't bother anybody, no one stopped them from sleeping there. The island was far from the collection of historical buildings just visible from the other side of the river. Across from him was the tail end of the city: ugly new apartments, a shopping mall, a small stadium. He was also visible when he was on the river island, and children sometimes waved and shouted to him from the embankment, asking for a ride in his canoe. The non-inventor would respond with enigmatic movements of his head. The attention of those children was flattering but also worrying. He didn't want them to discover what was happening to the rabbits, which could be glimpsed from the riverbank; they were like small white balls colliding with each other. At night, if there was a moon, the gleam of their coats could be mistaken for the white of the birds' plumage, giving the impression that the avians were sleeping on the ground.

The rabbits never ate their litters outside the tent. They seemed to know that they would be transgressing some law. And although the sight of the wretched beasts feeding on their babies was enough to shrivel his soul, when they were quiet it was evident that there was something hypnotic, majestic about them that increased with each passing day, and perhaps had to do with acting against nature. Maybe they have stopped being rabbits, he thought, or in some way know that they are caught up in a situation that is absolutely new to their species. From time to time the non-inventor mourned their mutation, and then he would manage to forget the circumstances surrounding their cannibalism. The whole thing would appear to be simple fact, without underlying causes; a fact that was inaugurating a new world. All this was happening in silence because there was still no language for a reality that was just taking its first steps. The non-inventor continued to visit the river island but did nothing more than cautiously respond to the pleas of the children for a ride in his canoe. At night, in the large house he'd inherited from his grandmother, he dreamed of the parents of those children, heard their voices like a mob crushing him, while the rooms of his home filled with water and the blue of swimming pools. He told himself it was a common obsession that would disappear once he'd made the decision to forget about the creatures; only a certain way of standing in a form of ecstasy when he was near the rabbits indicated that he was beginning to feel like one of them. Perhaps his rapidly graying hair would achieve the amazing whiteness of those now sacred animals, and his bloodshot eyes—the ophthalmologist said that the slight bleeds were due to chronic conjunctivitis—would be healed when they became completely red.

One day the non-inventor took down the tent and left the island. The people living in the apartments along the riverbank wondered what had happened to the crazy man who used to breed rabbits, all of which died a few weeks after his disappearance, their bodies forming a pretty white blanket over the island.

REGRESSION

The memory gushes in: She and Tamara at the age of ten with some dollhouses, several floors high, which could be opened down the middle. They were playing *The Colbys* or *Falcon Crest*, throwing dice to decide who got which clan and which mansion was going to be theirs. They used the slightly pompous word "mansion," which they had learned from the American series. In her hometown, no one referred to a house that way, no matter how luxurious it was. Although they had never seen anything even remotely similar to the mansions on *The Colbys* and *Falcon Crest*, when they imagined themselves as grown-ups they were always the owners of beautiful palaces standing by lakes and surrounded by wineries.

Another memory appears: Tamara leading her to La Calavera, a copse of very tall trees with a clearing in the middle where beggars sometimes slept. The children they used to have water bomb fights with said you could see decapitated birds in La Calavera first thing in the morning, and, according to their older brothers, satanic rituals were performed there. When the kids told them about the headless birds, just before filling their water bombs, Tamara laughed out loud, mocking them mercilessly, then whispered in her ear that there were no decapitated birds; what you could find there were weird animals from the center of the earth that had the ability to stay alive even when their body parts were separated. Their feet, torsos, and necks could hop around on their own.

They lived near the park that separated Espriu, with its wealthy families, from El Canal, a very old neighborhood bisected by an open sewer that poured its stinking contents into the sea. None of the relevant authorities would take responsibility for covering the sewer, and the rumor was that they all hoped the reek in the summer months along with the ruinous condition of the buildings would eventually prove too much for the residents. The authorities wanted to extend the main avenue of Espriu through El Canal to the sea. What actually happened was that, whenever an apartment was left empty after the death of the tenant, Romany people and junkies squatted there. In those days there were still a lot of junkies around.

Other memories appear: the afternoon she accompanied Tamara to her *iaia*'s house. Every day, she'd see the grandfather, a yarmulke on his bald head, collect Tamara after English class. They didn't attend a religious school, and when her friend confessed that her family was Jewish it gave her a strange feeling. There were so few Jews in Spain, it was as if her friend were special, a rare jewel.

Although she'd even gotten as far as speaking to her

42

friend's grandfather once or twice, it was a long time before she met the grandmother. Tamara tended to surround
her with an aura of reverence and mystery: "She can hardly
move," she'd say, "but she makes the best baked rice in the
whole city without getting out of her chair." Her friend
always made a big secret of having lunch with her grandmother. She'd only found out by asking bluntly. Tamara
finally said, "OK. Let's go to iaia's. But if you rat me out,
you're dead." She'd kept her mouth shut because visiting an
old lady didn't seem like a secret worth telling.

Her friend sneaked her into her iaia's home. She was
surprised that it was in El Canal, in one of the very old
buildings with blackened façades. That first impression
was nothing in comparison with what she saw at the end
of a terrazzo passage that didn't seem to fit with the peel-
ing, discolored wallpaper. The grandmother—an obese old
woman who smelled of burned eggplant—was floating,
motionless in a corner of the room by the curtain rail. She
had her back turned to them and was looking out into
the street. They crept across the room until they were di-
rectly below the grandmother. Her thighs were so fat that
from underneath all they could see were rolls of flab. The
soles of her small, perfectly formed feet were like those of
a child that has been flattened by the weight above. She
started to shiver, and Tamara spat out something defiant,
possibly spiteful. They backed out of the room, their eyes
fixed on the grandmother. When they were halfway across,
her friend bumped into a rocking chair. The grandmother
turned around and looked at them unsmilingly, as though
they were pieces of furniture. Tamara blushed bright red.

That afternoon, sitting in the park, her friend explained that the old woman floated because she was full of gas. "A gas that comes from the center of the earth." She refrained from asking how the iaia managed to cook the best baked rice in the whole city. Perhaps they had put the kitchen appliances on the ceiling. She was sorry not to have insisted on seeing the rest of the house, but on the other hand the idea of staying much longer in that place where everything was so grimy and stank of dried fish wasn't appealing.

How could she have forgotten it? How had an experience that should have made her doubt the whole of reality been substituted by another? Perhaps it had been so fantastic that she'd assimilated it into a dream. Perhaps its singularity had prevented her from processing it. Of the days after the visit, she remembered only pain. A hard, unspoken suffering. The next morning, when she boarded the school bus, Tamara was already there, sitting next to Juana; her friend didn't even look in her direction. Juana, a thin, grubby girl, who managed to avoid being ostracized by inventing gossip, gave her a malicious smile. From her seat, she spied on the two girls and was met with the spite of that bitter kid who wasn't content that Tamara had chosen her as a companion, but needed to rub it in. Her friend's metamorphosis seemed incredible: surely she had the right to pretend it hadn't happened. The way Tamara walked resolutely out of the classroom at recess, without once speaking to her or detaching herself from the huddle of other girls, the way she shared her chocolate croissant with them, should have been enough. But it wasn't. She tried behaving as if her friend were making a mistake. Couldn't she see that the others were just getting between them? Watching that pack of kids chewing their chocolate-filled croissants gave her an excuse for pulling Tamara away from those frauds. The words faded as they issued from her mouth: "They're using you." Only the "you"—a sort of pitiful grunt—was audible. The children fell silent and, in a loud, clear voice, Tamara said, "Can't you just go away and stop bothering me? You make me sick."

For months that "You make me sick" hung over her like a disgusting, shameful halo. In the past, she'd always been tough, but now she started to hide away, even trembling when her classmates pointed at her and whispered. Tamara's betrayal sank her in the typically sullen depression of girls who will never admit they are in the wrong. "Me, badly behaved? What the fuck are you talking about?" she shouted at her mom one day. And she got a slap across the face for that "fuck." For the rest of the school year she traveled alone.

She didn't hate her friend, just missed her. She watched her from a distance, hoping she wouldn't notice, and spent more time with the other marginalized girls in the class. There were various categories of marginalization: the fat, the geeky, the dull, the goody-goodies, the sneaks, the tomboys. Adolescence found her unsure which of those labels she'd been assigned, and in the habit of wandering aimlessly around the park that separated Espriu from El Canal. As the image of Tamara's grandmother floating in a corner of the living room had faded almost instantly from her memory, she never associated the snub with that event. On the other hand, she still remembers going to La Calavera in search of those disjointed creatures that, according to her friend, came from the center of the earth. All she found were used tissues, empty beer cans, and cigarette butts.

One night she came home late after binging on alcohol. Before turning onto the street where she lived, she stood quietly for a while on the edge of the park, her eyes peeled. She wanted to be sure that it was empty, that no one was watching her. There was no way she could be certain of either; the cabbage and sago palms at ground level, plus the thick trunks of the fig trees would provide cover for anyone who didn't want to be seen.

She headed for La Calavera, following the path she took almost every afternoon, and ducked through a gap in the undergrowth, from where she could see the moon, tinged yellow like a tooth coated with plaque. She was very frightened; certain that someone would be there. Someone who was waiting for her, and her alone. But that didn't prevent her from going on.

When her eyes had adapted to the dark she saw something glowing. It looked plastic but at the same time like living flesh. The thing moved slowly, making a hissing noise. She thought it might be a snake. A snake that was too rigid and thick. She ran.

Lying in her bed, everything throbbed.

The following morning she put it all down to drunken delusions.

Tamara spoke to her again when she turned eighteen. They bumped into one another at the window of a record shop. "I'm going in to buy *Portishead*," she said. "Do you want to come along?" They spent a long time standing in front of the "P" for Portishead repeated on the black sleeve and the screen on the back wall of the store. She liked the sound: Portishead. Portishead-Tamara: those names were linked for her. They went to the park and sat on the grass to continue their conversation about music and about when they used to play among those shrubs whose name had something to do with skulls. They didn't mention the six years of not talking to each other, as if everything that happened between the ages of twelve and eighteen had been erased. Then they walked into El Canal. Some of the older houses were *okupas* now, squats. Beer and *calimocho* were for sale in the front yards and ska music was playing. They finally ventured into one of the okupas, and after a few drinks went to another, which was on the street where Tamara's grandparents had lived. She would have sworn that it was even the same building.

Her memory of the day they had visited Tamara's iaia was vague. It included a dish of baked rice that an obese woman who wasn't floating near the ceiling served to Tamara's parents, siblings, and grandfather—not wearing his yarmulke—at a table that filled so much of the living room it was impossible to go to the bathroom until after dessert without everyone having to get up. She has no idea what they did afterward, or why she'd even had lunch with Tamara's grandparents. The images froze there, the aftertaste of garlic, potatoes, and beans mixed with the rice and the iaia's bulging calves. As if the old woman's legs were basic ingredients of the dish.

The okupa was a two-story building with a terrace and patches of dirty blue and white tiles on the façade. In recent years, whenever she'd passed through El Canal—heading north to the market gardens rather than to the beach—she scrupulously avoided this side street. If she ever accidentally found herself at the intersection, she ran in the opposite direction, her eyes fixed on the ground, convinced that her refusal to look would save her from an encounter with Tamara. Her incursions into El Canal had nothing to do with her friend; what interested her was the neighborhood's reputation, a notoriety whose origins were lost in time (within the short time of her own life, in fact). Apparently its inhabitants possessed certain qualities not shared by the rest of the population, and on more than one occasion she'd followed someone, hoping that their journey through the narrow backstreets would reveal something beyond her reach. A secret city. Bodies from the rock or from the sea.

"We could take a look around the whole okupa," said Tamara. They had crossed the threshold into a kind of large foyer surrounded by rooms without doors; the size made her doubt if it had ever been the home of her friend's paternal grandparents. The brief scene filed away in her memory had been played out in a small, airless room. Had the house perhaps been inhabited by a number of tenants? Did poor families live, piled one on top of the other, in the former summer villas of the well-to-do? She knew nothing about the neighborhood. Why had she spent more time imagining what it was like than reading up on its history?

They were sitting on tiny stools on a patio with planters

in which a few vegetables grew among the withered weeds. On the upper floor, they could see more people on a terrace with paper lanterns, candles, and although they had the impression that it wasn't open to customers—for the simple reason that no one had shown them how to reach it—they thought that it would be a good place to begin their exploration. Without asking permission, they walked through the dark rooms until they found the stairs.

She was certain then that it really was the house where her friend's grandparents had lived, and that it was the second time she'd been in this place whose essence had been razed to the ground but was still alive. The grandfather with his yarmulke and the iaia were standing on a step somewhere or sitting in the bright eastern light of one of the bedrooms, the lace curtains fluttering in the breeze.

The staircase was steep and there were chips in the terrazzo. A strip of light filtering under the doorway at the top might be coming from a room it would be better not to enter: probably the same one she had preserved in her memory. She didn't ask herself why she put such value on that vague, uninteresting memory; eating a meal with her friend's family, mild astonishment at a pair of fat legs.

They opened the door cautiously because they could hear nothing from the other side. A blank wall of silence had fallen between them when they reached the head of the stairs. They pushed the door, expecting to find someone sleeping or undressed, but what they found was the terrace; the looks the people gave them made it clear they weren't welcome. The area must be reserved for the residents of the okupa. A girl—the embodiment of El Canal

49

punk—with a crest of red hair, wearing a black top, plaid skirt, and ripped stockings pierced by safety pins said, "You looking for someone?" Their jaws dropped at the sight of her. El Canal punk girls had leading roles in the stories told in the schoolyard. "He was mugged by an El Canal punk girl;" "She left home and became an El Canal punk girl;" "He's dating an El Canal punk girl." They had seen punk girls from a distance on Friday evenings in the Rambla, where the bars frequented by high school seniors were located. But this was the first time they had viewed one close up, one who—what's more—was talking to them. Their dumbstruck awe gave way to the shame of not being able to come up with an answer. You could tell a mile off that they were two nice young Espriu girls. Thoroughly embarrassed, they turned and left, and it was only after they had been walking for a while, starting to enjoy the quiet of the streets, that she found the courage to ask her friend if her iaia had once lived in that okupa.

Tamara gave a loud laugh.

"Are you out of your mind?" After a silence her friend continued: "My grandparents had an apartment in Benicalap. Don't you remember when you came to lunch there?"

It had been only a couple of hours since the wake of that meal had washed up against her, but she was still unable to speak of it. Suddenly it no longer felt like a vestige of something real. She had the strong impression that she'd invented the whole thing. The idea that Tamara might be participating in the farce terrified her.

"I'm going home."

Her friend oozed disdain. There was a note of sarcasm in her voice when she said:

"Don't you want to see my grandparents' apartment?"

They walked south through El Canal, holding their noses when they passed the open sewer. The occasional old summer villas interspersed among fishermen's cottages gave way to three-story brick buildings. She wanted to turn, to leave Tamara on her own, but continued to follow her, as though they were walking through a long narrow gorge instead of along city streets. She fixed her eyes on her friend's back, the long mane of black hair, or on the ground so as not to trip. The sidewalks seemed unusually dark, and once or twice she almost fell flat on her face, not because of the cracks in the pavement, but from the sensation that she'd come across an unexpected step. That feeling—which lasted the milliseconds it took her foot to find solid ground, and made her body think it had dropped into a hole, an abyss—also had its origin in Tamara's long, thick hair. She was scared that her friend would turn around and have a different face, the features of that fat, deformed grandmother who had floated in the air—a fact that she suddenly remembered. Her fear contrasted with the peaceful night. It was past one in the morning and the bars were closing. Groups of people who had come out for dinner were slowly disappearing, like the embers of a cigarette thrown on the ground. They came to a square where some boys were sitting on the curb, drinking from large plastic cups. They whistled as the two girls passed.

"That was my grandparents' apartment," said Tamara, pointing to a long, narrow rather depressing balcony.

"I must have gotten muddled," she replied.

The impression of madness or that Tamara was pulling her leg vanished.

That summer they wandered together through the empty city, never thinking that it was the last time they would be together in those deserted summer streets in just that way. On a number of occasions they explored El Canal, walking along the dirt tracks in the orchards that wound down to the beach, where trash was burned in the late afternoon and everything was clouded by a layer of bluish smoke. Only bikers and dogs haunted such god-forsaken places. Once or twice they ventured into other neighborhoods to see what they were like with the stores closed—it was mid August and midweek—and the dim orange streetlighting filtering through the leaves of plain trees in the smooth humidity. They never sweated. They were at that age when the body deals more easily with heat than cold, and they spent that month alone. Their parents and siblings were on vacation for the month. They bought marijuana and smoked it in a *tasca* where reefer was allowed, and then they bared their souls to each other, lying on the grass in the park with a liter bottle of beer that was always too warm, and from which they only drank to quench their thirst.

That August was as intense as a whole childhood. Then September arrived with the parents and other people. They saw each other secretly and never told their respective circles of friends about their meetings at the entrance to La Calavera, from which came the murmured rustling of something dragging itself along the ground. She'd call up the image of the creatures Tamara had described years before—something like lizard tails—and also, above all, the fat old woman. The question still burned on her lips.

They went to different universities. Her friend chose psychology, while she studied humanities. For a while they telephoned and arranged to meet occasionally on a Sunday, until Tamara moved to another neighborhood and they lost track of one another.

PARIS PÉRIPHÉRIE

I don't like using maps. I'm sort of dyslexic about them and unless I really concentrate, I get the streets mixed up so that when I'm trying to find, let's say, Ocean Square, I walk in the opposite direction, toward Island Avenue. It's because I confuse the names, not the direction. My memory puts them in different places. So I'm surprised to find myself going the wrong way—because my intuition, which I never follow, is usually right—but even then I tell myself that Ocean Square is somewhere nearby, that I've seen it on the map. And so I walk on, ignoring the signs and following some crazy route.

Today is one of those days when there's no option but to consult a map. I've just alighted at Carrefour Pleyel and I'm trying to find the Social and Administrative Center for the northern peripheral suburbs. Tomorrow is the deadline for the CAF, a grant that will allow me to continue living in a residency in Mairie de Saint-Ouen for another six months. I take careful note of the platform, as I always do when I get off at a station for the first time, despite the fact that they all look the same to me. The exit is on Avenue Anatole-France, which to judge by the number of the center—345—has to be very long.

I walk through an underpass to get to the odd numbers. At the level of the metro there are a few cafés, and then a hotel—number 357. The avenue is, indeed, interminable; looking south from where I stand, I can't see its end. The buildings are ugly; Soviet era, with dismal, murky colors. When I reach a white brick house on a corner I feel a storm coming. The incredibly dry mildew on the walls, the lush vegetation of the overgrown garden, and the rain give me a sense of alienation that I've experienced before.

The number of the house is printed so large that at first I take it for something else. It's on a red plaque hanging on the iron gate: 323. Under the plaque is an orange sign attached by bits of wire that says FOR SALE. It dawns on me that there are seventeen numbers missing, so I turn and make my way around a traffic circle. I have no idea which way to go. A street with three cold, modern skyscrapers leads from Anatole-France; none of them look like they might be the location of the Social and Administrative Center. But I'm not ready to give up.

It begins to rain. I work out that the skyscrapers aren't in fact on the street, but up a ramp that veers off to the left. The street continues on to a freeway. The neighborhoods of the northern periphery stretch out into the distance; they are depressing watered-down replicas of Carrefour Pleyel, yet during the brief instant while I'm gazing at them I have a vaguely pleasurable sense of unease. I think I might need to cross the freeway to reach the stretch of avenue I want, but for the moment I opt for the ramp. I advance. There are no street signs; I'm certain that I'm heading nowhere. I continue to advance. When I get to the skyscrapers, I discover that they are surrounded by a parking lot full of trucks.

Option two: cross the freeway. I take the street; it comes to an abrupt end at an embankment. I stand there observing the maelstrom of traffic passing at exhausting speed under the rain. My shoes are soaked. When I get back to my tiny room at the residency I phone Michel and get his voicemail message in French. In my diary I write: "Even if I return every day, I'll never find the place." That's not enough to get the whole thing off my chest. I go to my bookshelves and find a collection of articles by Marguerite Duras called *Outside*. I know that one of those articles is about the Paris suburbs. I read that there are no maps of the periphery. That it's impossible to draw them up. That they only exist for the old neighborhoods like Saint-Denis, before the construction of the *banlieues*. Banlieues: the exact opposite of empty Paris boulevards from which the Arabs, treated like rats by their white neighbors, have fled.

By the next day I've forgotten my misgivings and set off along the odd numbers, determined to ask. I approach an elderly woman who tells me that I don't have to leave the underpass because the center is at the end of a passage that branches off from the exit to the even numbers. I can't miss it.

I cross the avenue and walk down the even numbers. There's no passage. Then I try the underpass to the odds.

I retrace my steps to the concourse and go back onto the platform. I know it's absurd, but you never know. Worn out, I ask again. Three people give the same answer: they don't know where the center is, and I should return to the street and ask there. On the street, I've had it with asking. I call Michel from a public telephone.

"For goodness sake," he says, "it's right by the exit!"

"I can't see it. Where were you yesterday? Where have you been for the last five days? I said I'd probably be calling you for help."

"Where are you?"

"I just told you."

"Can you see a glass building opposite the metro?"

"There's no glass building. Where have you been?"

"Yes there is. Are you sure you're at Carrefour Pleyel? Under the Pleyel Tower?"

"I'm under the Pleyel Tower."

"So maybe I've got it wrong. Let me think. Do you want me to come there? I'm sure I'll remember when I see it."

"Where were you yesterday?"

"I'm not answering that. Today's the deadline, and if you want us to be together you'd better get a move on."

"I know."

"Wait for me. I'll be there in half an hour."

"I don't want you to come."

I hang up. I have no more coins. It's over. I think that I don't think about Michel, that I've never in my whole life thought about him. Or better: that in the time I have left on this earth he's not even going to be a memory. I have memories of cows and sheep. Even of pulsating green gobs on the sidewalk. But of him, zilch. No memories. I'd like to shout that out loud and laugh. It's a frightening coldness, a liberating coldness. I'm on the point of leaving when I take a last look at what lies beyond the freeway. Just as happened the day before, the sight of Saint-Denis shrouded in fog produces a jolt that seesaws between fascination and dread. I tell myself that I can take a stroll into that vision I find so attractive and if I happen to come across the center I can ring Michel and say that I've found it, but that I'm leaving. That I've got all the documents for the grant in my hands, and that I'm sitting on the toilet about to piss on them.

I look around with the all-seeing attention of a sleep-walker. The first stretch of the walkway to the other side of the freeway is a path that runs steeply down a gulley and under a concrete bridge. The noise of the cars, trapped and amplified by the bridge, is thunderous. I run, trip. The path peters out into grass and I have to ascend a steep bank and jump a low wall whose presence there in the middle of nowhere, next to a gulley, doesn't seem to relate to any civilization. More paths lead out from this wasteland and behind is the freeway, the chaos of the whole world. I don't need to get closer to know that I'm not going to find anything here. Empty stretches of land with huge billboards, a junkyard, a used car lot surrounded by barbed wire, full of small flags flapping frenetically in the wind. Silent, non-functioning factories. About seven hundred meters away the city reappears. I see the signs of supermarkets, the small stores from which emerge women carrying packages.

I don't even bother to look at the street numbers. I go back down under the bridge, where I wait until the noise and the certainty of being about to lose it become unbearable. When I get out of here, I say to myself in an attempt to get back the thread, when I get out of here, I'll call Michel and tell him to come and help me.

MYOTRAGUS

She deftly carved a slice of the meat and put it in her mouth. Even before doing so, she'd scowled, as though she'd already decided that there was something highly questionable in the appearance of the roast meat. He took no notice; after all, she'd spent the whole weekend turning up her nose at everything. That morning, while they were waiting for the walk signal on the Gran Vía de Colón, she'd slipped her hand into his pocket. A few of her acquaintances greeted her and she thrust her hand deeper into his overcoat, clenching her fist. Maybe she wanted him to protect her from those people: a couple, both local government employees, who eyed her suspiciously; a neighbor who gave him a vaguely knowing look. He found a way to hold that tightly clenched fist. Her unexpected fear was endearing; it reminded him of his daughter when she was just a few years old and something—a dog, another child—would terrify her. When that happened, he'd pick her up and hug her, but the small fists clinging to his shoulder would never unclench. Other than his daughter, he'd never known anyone who kept their fear in their fists. The fact that she shared some character traits with his child felt like a good omen. But that illusion was short lived: when the acquaintances were gone she took her hand out of his pocket. She'd just been showing them that she was dating someone, and the clenched fist was really a sign that she didn't want to hold his hand.

"This isn't kid goat," she now said.

He was putting on his glasses; these days he wasn't capable of eating without them. He took his time before sampling the meat. The woman put two more pieces in her mouth, chewed, and swallowed, all the while shaking her head. He quickly took a bite of the meat to check if she was right before the waiter she had called over could arrive at their table.

"This isn't kid goat," she said tartly.

It occurred to him that, like his wife, who had died the year before, she always needed to be the center of attention.

"That's top quality kid goat, señora," replied the waiter.

"No it isn't. I know kid goat when I see it. I've eaten it often and always cook it at home when my children visit. It's perfectly clear to me that this isn't kid goat."

"I can show you the carcass."

"I'm already looking at the piece of meat that interests me. What you've got in the freezer is your own affair."

"We can offer you something else if you want."

"What I want is a plastic bag. I work in a laboratory and I'm going to analyze this meat. If it isn't kid goat, I'll complain to the authorities. This man will be my witness."

She pointed an accusing finger, as if he too were pretending to be kid goat.

The waiter went in search of a plastic bag.

"I hope it doesn't have any holes," she said when the bag was brought, and then she dropped the leg of kid goat into it.

She rolled the bag up tightly and placed it in her purse. When they left the restaurant, once she'd explained how she was going to carry out the analysis of the sample and proudly informed him of how often the careful work undertaken by her laboratory had exposed restaurants—as many as seven cases where the meat wasn't what was claimed on the menu—he said that as far as he was concerned it was kid goat. She made no reply and they didn't exchange another word until he decided to leave for his home in another city. When they got to his car, she confessed that she'd been alone for too long. She was nervous. But in any case, she was going to analyze the meat.

The Majorcan mouse-goat died out some five thousand years ago. Its form has been recreated in drawings and there was even a wine whose label included a very free interpretation of the extinct animal. The illustration on the bottles was reminiscent of some kind of diabolical billy goat, or an aged satyr who harries women and is capable of appearing suddenly at night, like a ghost. It is believed that the mouse-goat was a food source for Neolithic humans due to the number of bones found in caves; this leads to the supposition that its flesh had a pleasant flavor. Scientists think it probable that the extinction of the mouse-goat was caused by the huge appetite of Neolithic man. It is also known that, being confined to the island of Majorca, the Balearic mouse-goat had difficulty finding food. In order to adapt to the scarcity of resources it became reptilian: it evolved into a cold-blooded animal and changed its growth rate and metabolism to make the most efficient use of the available vegetation. An adult mouse-goat weighed about thirteen kilos, was approximately fifty centimeters tall, and had short back legs. It was not a nimble animal, and had no need to be: it had no predators on the archipelago. Except for man, of course. Its brain was small, which meant it moved slowly. It used sunlight as a source of energy, as lizards do, and its head would seem strange to us nowadays as its eye sockets were set on the front of its face rather than to the sides; it also had a short snout and a grotesque jaw.

Standing on the terrace of the *muntanyeta*, Archduke Peter John was deeply concerned about the *myotragus*. In the early hours of the previous day an animal had jumped out in front of him while he was walking to the cliffs. It was still dark, but the archduke was in the habit of taking his constitutional before sunrise, and was even able to make his way with his eyes closed without straying onto the paths of the land adjoining Son Moragues, such as the one that offered a view of the sea below. He'd honed his night vision and enjoyed practicing the skill when the sky was overcast and there was no moon. In such conditions he would sometimes make out strange movements in the bark of trees: the furrows moved laterally to form cracks he never found the courage to inspect up close. He knew that those cracks didn't contain smooth wood, that they weren't the live flesh of the trunk, but deep chasms that would swallow him whole. The movements of the bark made him think of armies of marching ants. Suddenly, the forest was overrun by every member of the *formicidae* family found on his travels to wilder, more torrid regions. He would be forced to lower his eyes as there was always a moment when the dance of the trees closed in on him and he felt those perhaps illusory ants surrounding him, ready to crawl up his legs.

But what had happened the day before was different. As he approached a stretch of the path edged with broom, with the tang of salt already in the air, an animal appeared from the undergrowth that bore no resemblance to the irrational sights the archduke had learned to see. This animal was definitely real and, despite the darkness, he realized that it was looking at him. The creature didn't belong to any known species. It wasn't a wild boar, a goat, a sheep, or a hare, and definitely not a dog. In addition to its outlandish form, the archduke had been astonished to note that its movements were just as awkward as his own. The animal crossed the path slowly and disappeared into the bushes, giving the archduke time to think that he and the beast must have the same medical condition.

He suffered from elephantiasis. His custom—known only to a few—of walking at night or sleeping outdoors on one of the terraces of his estate, listening to the nocturnal sounds, was related to his illness. The elephantiasis made him walk differently from other people, and he felt protected from their gazes in the darkness. It took him hours to reach the clifftop, but no one was watching. He was free to go as slowly as he needed. Nicanor, his deaf and dumb servant, would drive him back to Son Moragues in a buggy pulled at a trot by an Andalusian horse. They were always back home before sunrise. It wasn't easy to communicate with Nicanor, but the man had found a way of making himself understood and never gossiped, as had happened with the other deaf mutes who'd been in his service. The archduke was loved for giving employement to deaf mutes, among other things; many people thought of him as a benefactor and idealist, although an equal number hated him.

This servant, who seemed to commune with his master in a secret language, also carried out certain dubious tasks. On occasion the archduke would ask him to recruit a couple of girls. The deaf-mute would travel to the other end of the island to choose two adolescents from the most poverty-stricken classes. While everyone was sleeping, the girls would wait naked in a clearing in the woods, with stones tied to their ankles to prevent them from running. The archduke's game was to hunt them. They dragged themselves along until he caught them, at which point Nicanor would appear and join the orgy. The next day the unfortunate girls, with rope burns on their legs and blood-stained thighs, would be returned to their families along with provisions, money, and a letter of recommendation in the archduke's own hand attesting to their suitability for employment in the households of wealthy local families.

But that day, on the terrace of the muntanyeta, not even the memory of his most debauched nights could compete with his astonishment at the sight of the animal, whose name he now knew, or thought he knew: myotragus.

He'd learned about that extinct species on a visit to London's National History Museum, where he was shown the preserved bones of the creature; a hybrid, he understood, of a goat and a mouse. Dorothea Bate, the paleontologist who discovered the first fossil remains, told him that it had died out thousands of years ago. The archduke had also viewed a number drawings based on the skeleton of the mouse-goat, which stood with humble majesty in its glass case. Those drawings obsessed him. He was fascinated by everything related to Majorca and, since his arrival on the island, had paid ethnologists and geologists to carry out research there. He himself had made not a few excursions to broaden his knowledge of the terrain and had written books on the Balearics. Only autochthonous plants grew there, and he employed botanists to catalogue the flora on the whole island. He made wine from the grapes and pressed oil from the olives found in no other region, and had even founded an agricultural museum. He commissioned landscapes from the artists who took up residence in S'Estaca for long periods, and demanded such levels of faith to nature that the paintings could be mistaken for their real counterparts. He'd also invited paleontologists, ornithologists, biologists, and even the famous naturalist Odón de Buen; in his house in Miramar, the two of them had lengthy discussions about the theory of the origin of the species. The archduke had believed that everything was catalogued and ready to be exhibited to his guests, as if the whole island were a showcase. He was openly proud of what he'd done for Majorca. But the animal that had crossed his path in the night, with its gait so similar to the withered limp of the elephantiasis sufferer, wounded that pride.

He considered ordering his servants to search the Serra de Tramuntana, but was deterred by the thought that what he had seen was just the product of delirium, and that people might begin to talk.

He decided to wait until the creature made another appearance. He had no idea whether the myotragus was nocturnal or diurnal, and so he increased the frequency of his walks. One night, when his deaf-mute servant had brought him two young girls, he found himself incapable of doing anything beyond sitting on a rock pretending to observe how Nicanor dealt with them. He was, in fact, looking into the undergrowth and on three occasions— when he heard a noise—rose to search among the mastic trees. He also paid a little more attention to the girls. He felt like a lecherous old man with ridiculously extravagant tastes. That is perhaps why he ordered Nicanor to take them to the kitchen in Son Moragues and offer them the leftovers of the kid goat they had eaten for lunch, so that they would at least not feel pangs of hunger on their return journey. Neither the other staff nor his guests—an acclaimed Nicaraguan poet and a choreographer who was working on a dance extravaganza to celebrate the archduke's honorary citizenship—were surprised to see them. It seemed that everyone on the estate had witnessed his bacchanals, and assessed the adolescents as they might a

Majorcan sausage. He later learned that the slimmer of the two girls had begged a maid to help her to remain there in service:

"We're very poor, and I won't be able to marry now," she'd said.

The maid talked to the housekeeper, who passed on the message to the archduke.

"Very well," he replied. "But I don't want her anywhere near me. Send her to S'Estaca and tell her to hold her tongue about how she came to be here."

He feared becoming the laughingstock of the estate. How much was known about his sexual proclivities? Was his servant really to be trusted? He'd never seen Nicanor communicate with anyone else, but that was possibly one of his talents. He might very well have formed alliances with the housekeeper or the overseer. He imagined them all—helped by his servants—hidden among the trees, shrieking with surprise and glee at the antics of that old man with deformed legs.

On the following nights he took the path to the cliffs and stopped at the point where the mouse-goat had suddenly appeared. He stood there for over an hour on each occasion, but his patience was never rewarded. He even began to think that he'd lost his ability to see the nocturnal movements in the forest. The bark of the holm oaks held nothing more than patches of dry moss and only a few wild goats broke the monotony of the wearisome silence. On those nights, when he came to the end of the path, he would take the track along the clifftop, cobbled with granite. The stones seemed to form a natural lane. He'd constructed a simple lookout on the west-ernmost end of the lane, with seats made from boulders where he could rest his swollen legs. Almost despairing, he contemplated the dark mass of the sea with a waning moon above its gently stirring waters. Although the Mediterranean was never menacing, he felt a dread of being there alone. Resisting the urge to throw himself down onto the rocks, he continued to observe the cliffs, the blackness of the Mediterranean, and the gentle mist. Given his elephantiasis, what could the future hold for him but immobility?

Dawn was breaking: the cliffs no longer urged him to suicide. He got into the buggy and dozed until they reached the house. Then he ate a hearty breakfast of eggs and sausage, asking himself what should be done about the mouse-goat. He bought two hundred kids and ordered the servants to fatten them for several days before freeing the gleaming animals into the estate at nightfall. On five successive nights he went out with Nicanor and a shotgun. Since his adolescence, hunting had been an addiction. He'd killed stags, elephants, roe deer, gazelles, and boar. The kids ran behind the wild nanny goats, attempting to find ones that would feed them, but the goats kicked them away, and very soon there were groups of exhausted young creatures beneath the trees. They also showed a proclivity to follow the humans. After hours hunting for the myotragus, the archduke dispatched each of the kids with a single shot. His dismay deepened with the passing days, and he hosted sumptuous parties in a number of the surrounding villages where roast meat was served to the guests. After his death, rumor spread across the island that the extinction of the myotragus was due to the archduke's habit of feeding it to the young girls he'd courted.

NOTES ON THE ARCHITECTURE
OF HELL

I will ascend into heaven, I will exalt my throne above the stars
of God: I will sit also upon the mount of the congregation,
in the sides of the north: I will ascend above the heights
of the clouds; I will be like the most High.

—ISAIAH 14:13–14 (K.J.V.)

1

There was no park in the vicinity but the air still smelled of earth. Just over two kilometers away was La Almudena Cemetery, and he thought the emanations of the dead hovered over the whole city.

Madrid was full of cemeteries. San Isidro, the Parroquial in Carabanchel Bajo, the British Cemetery, beautiful if only for its peculiarities: it had no grass and was overlooked by the backs of dilapidated buildings with a network of clotheslines, on which hung underwear whose various sizes and colors seemed to suggest elderly residents. And then there were the cemeteries that had disappeared, such as the Sacramental de San Martín in Vallehermoso or the Norte in Arapiles (now the site of a branch of El Corte Inglés), where bodies had found their final resting place until the early twentieth century.

He was ashamed of his profession, but that was

nothing new. In the eighties, he'd left his job as an urban planner at City Hall to travel to Central America. He'd ended up in Mexico, suffering from psychosis after a blurry five months of shamans and peyote. He never told anyone that he'd been admitted to a psychiatric clinic because he was convinced that some green xoloitzcuintle dogs were talking to him in the language of his whole family: his grandmother, his uncle, his unborn brothers and sisters, the words of Older Brother. While he liked urban planning, the thought of going back to City Hall, to the same job as before, was almost more than he could bear; his colleagues looking at him askance because they hated the fact that he'd had the courage to leave, and the nerve to return and use his contacts to get back his old position and salary. During that period his senses developed a new faculty that made him stop in the middle of the street because he'd heard a whisper in his ear or felt a persistent warmth on his left shoulder—a warmth that didn't originate in his flesh or bones, but came from outside and had the physical presence of a hand, even though there was nothing on his collarbone but a dark red polo shirt and that persistent sensation. The first voice he clearly heard, coming from every corner of the silent house, frightened him because he guessed that he was going to start having delusions, that it was going to be an absurd repetition of the xoloitzcuintles. But that cold analysis was proof that it was something else, something non-delusional. Then he started to think differently—that's to say, without resentment—about Older Brother—by then dead for more than twenty years—about the stigma the family never mentioned, about how

he too, the favorite younger brother, had lived through everything that happened with equal shame, and how he'd
never stopped dogging his elder brother's footsteps, reading his favorite books, looking at his photographs, playing his music (since his death he'd slept with his record
collection under his bed). It was all due to an obsession or
something in his genes. Long, empty years went by before
he was able to admit that to himself; as if his interest was
of some different nature, a simple question of affinity, even
justice. He remembers the day he saw Older Brother lose
his mind. The memory was clear, precise: a fall afternoon,
a pale brown church on the corner, the leaves of the plane
trees on the sidewalks. Older Brother climbing a streetlight, chanting a passage from the Apocalypse at the top of
his lungs. He looked possessed; he'd shaved his head with
a knife, making nicks all over his scalp. The blood was still
glistening like a fresh flower, like the gash in the side of
Jusepe de Ribera's *Tityos*.

But in fact, things had begun to go wrong before
that, when his brother went away for a whole year. His
mother had covered up for him. Suddenly toys started to
arrive. A Scalextric. Cowboys and Indians. Jump ropes.
A Dulcita doll for the little girl. Santa Claus stopped by
his home every two or three weeks; Santa Claus was his
brother. "Your brother was here last night," his mother
would say. "But he had to go. It was really late and you
were already in bed. He's working very hard right now,
but he brought you this." Laurita fell for it, swallowed the
whole story about those things being presents from an
invisible brother, a cutout brother, a hopscotch brother, a

Hula-Hoop brother, a Rin Tin Tin brother, "Wake us up next time, Mommy." He, however, had been trusted with the secret. "I've got an important mission. I have to leave." That farewell on a Sunday at six in the morning had been no dream, even if his mother's charade might suggest otherwise. But he didn't have the courage to contradict her. It was as if he were obliged to believe them both, believe that the two explanations could coexist: leaving and being here in a ghostly way, like something nocturnal, invisible, that only appeared at specific times. Two years later, after three months of sporadic visits, of turning up for breakfast, for instance, or to take them out on a cold evening in a hired Dodge Dart—before that he'd come in a black Mercedes, sometimes with a driver—and travel through the night to an icy dawn in Roncesvalles, he suffered a full-blown bout of insanity. He saw giant beetles, thought a man was following him. He used to recite from books. To his parents' shock, he moved back into the house, and when he wasn't smashing his fists into the furniture or lowering the blinds because he'd spotted the person who was trying to catch him, he'd be howling with laughter or dissolving packets of Chino Mandarín flan in the bathtub. He, for his part, believed Older Brother's claim that someone was spying on them, and thought it was fun to see him taking a bath in flan mix, singing *The Phillipics* in Latin and talking to invisible people. When his brother climbed the streetlight with a strength and agility that bore no relationship to his scrawny frame and was then taken away in an ambulance, he couldn't understand why no one was suspicious, why they didn't look behind the hedges to see if someone was lurking there, why they didn't get a medium to check if the house was haunted. He searched carefully among the cypresses and demanded silence at the turn in the hallway where his brother had held conversations with the voices. But he never saw or heard anything. The house was dead and his brother also seemed to have died. His mother moved around like a shadow. Her time was spent between her bed and the couch, she didn't give orders to the domestic staff, scarcely ate, and their aunt Puri came to live with them. Puri took them to school, and in the evenings made them sit still for three hours to do their homework. Even his sister, who was too young for homework, didn't stir from her chair as she filled the pages of her exercise book. Each day their aunt repeated that what had happened to their brother was the result of a pact with the Devil. Once their mother was capable of doing something other than lying on the bed or the couch, she had an argument with their aunt and Puri packed her bags, never to return. Then one morning, their grandmother Carmen woke them:

"Your parents are going to take a vacation," she told them. "I'll stay here with you until they come back."

Neither he nor his sister missed their parents. Their departure coincided with summer and the end of classes, and they had both had more than enough melodrama. Plus they were too young to ask questions: they didn't even know that Older Brother wasn't their father's son; that their mother had secretly given birth to him while still almost a child herself, and for a long time had referred to her son as if he were also her brother. As if Older Brother were everybody's brother. And they didn't notice their father's relief at being rid of that illegitimate son, that person who had gone on living at home well into adulthood, beyond what was reasonable, who looked old enough to be his wife's husband and the father of their children, and was the consequence of pure evil.

Even before he was admitted to the psychiatric clinic in Mexico, during that whole year Older Brother was missing, he'd lived out a fantasy that put a positive slant on his brother's absence. At the time of his birth, Older Brother had been a senior official in the Ministry of Defense, and was then later appointed director of NASA's Apollo tracking station in Fresnedillas de la Olivia. Although he was still just a small child when his brother worked at the ministry, he remembered the grave expressions of certain visitors, and also the ban on talking about his brother's job. ("Just say he's in business." But he never took any notice of that; all the kids in his class knew that he had a brother who was much older and very important.) There were nights when Older Brother didn't come home and their mother slept by the telephone, which rang every time the radio gave the hour, as if announcing the outbreak of war or an attack by enemy nations. That was the time of the official car, the black Mercedes with a driver that turned up on weekdays, which was a great source of speculation about just what his brother's exceptional responsibilities might be. When he began to work for NASA, he compensated for not being able to discuss his job with stories about other planets, astronauts, and flying saucers, like the unidentified object that crashed to earth on a farm in New

Mexico—Older Brother had shown him a photo of it in a UFO magazine—and the two hundred students who'd seen a spaceship descend onto a hayfield in Australia. The move from there to connecting his absence to some investigation he was in charge of and that required his complete attention was very simple for a child, and desirable to the extent that it exempted his beloved brother from the blame for the long evenings of mute renunciation. What's more, that disappearance coincided with a UFO phenomenon that was so widely reported in the press and on television he became a news-bulletin junky. And, for the first time, he began to read newspapers. He searched for more information about the sightings that had the whole country on tenterhooks, on the verge of religious mania, since there were people who asserted that it was angels not Martians landing on earth. It was so lovely to imagine his brother beneath the four round lights that, night after night, hovered like birds over the bell tower of a village church. The locals had been evacuated and the zone cordoned off; on the television you could watch soldiers—still in black and white—pointing their weapons at reporters and gawkers who traveled there from all points of the peninsula. The papers printed daily statements by UFO experts. He remembered one individual from Valladolid who claimed to have traveled the world following sightings, and said that the glowing spheres were triangular spacecraft with white jet streams.

2

He and his sister began to visit Older Brother every Saturday; it was like being with an extraterrestrial. On some of their earliest visits to the clinic a nurse led them to the garden, where he'd be waiting for them, dozing in the sun. He no longer told them anything about himself, just asked questions that they answered like people making a report, anxious to include every single detail to avoid the inevitable silence that would follow. After a while the conversation became almost natural, if somewhat mentally disordered.

Despite his hatred of his stepson, it was their father who had convinced their mother to let them visit. Five years after Older Brother entered the clinic their father sat him and his sister down and, with the help of a book about mental illnesses bought specifically for this purpose, explained their brother's condition. The book had been placed on a shelf in the study as one more reference text. The very first meeting took place under the supervision of one of the medical staff, in a very hot room. The swollen, obtuse man his brother had become made him uncomfortable; he watched them without saying a word, then told them that one of the inmates was stealing his cigarettes and that he didn't like having to take a shower in hot water. They walked around the garden in contrite silence; it took Older Brother over an hour to realize that his behavior was inappropriate. When they were saying goodbye, he gave them some muddled, disinterested recommendations, as though in some part of his hippocampus, family ties were struggling to get through but couldn't find a foothold.

At first he thought that the intellectual and emotional paralysis, that stupefied-lump-of-flesh state, was the product of illness, but then he read up on the side effects of the pills and started to wonder who his brother would be without all that chemically induced equanimity. It was something he'd have to work out for himself. Careful observation of his brother's gestures and facial expressions led only to an understanding of the futility of observing a drugged patient. When they stayed for a meal at the clinic, Laurita, who had grown into a brash girl, treated Older Brother in a way he himself found humiliating; she'd wipe his face with a napkin, reprimand him when his peas rolled off the plate onto the table. He tried to act as if Older Brother's brain wasn't anesthetized by Haloperidol, attempting to find topics of conversation that would reactivate some connection in his brain. He still firmly believed that everything depended on finding some switch that would lead them to an understanding of him, and one day he concluded that it was the drugs that were causing the greatest harm. He wrongly assumed that this dire situation wouldn't involve any other changes in their daily lives, but after a bout of depression, his mother began to act as though she'd never given birth to her older son. She moved the furniture around in his room and threw out all his belongings. They were living between Calle Isaac Peral and Paseo de Juan XXIII, in one of those detached, upper-class houses near the best schools, university buildings, and leafy parks from the Franco era; whenever he walked through the clump of trees that separated Isaac Peral from the school of medicine, he'd feel that Madrid's wealthy Sierra Norte area began there, and that he could reach out and touch the peaks of the still densely forested mountains. The air in those mountains was so pure that it was recommended for tuberculosis sufferers. They had a swimming pool that was covered in winter, and that, by the time June came around, was a wriggling mass of scum and tadpoles. There was a garden with a pergola, rose beds, three chestnut trees, and cypress hedges that grew higher than the two-meter street wall. But despite all this, it had taken him a long time to recognize his privilege. First, because he only mixed with children of his own class, and then because he experienced the absence of his brother, his insanity, and his mother's detachment as a sort of homelessness.

3

By 1972, the year his father bought him a Mini to celebrate his brilliant grades and choice of major—architecture—his differences from the rest of the family had become more marked. He used to site his dark skin, his permanent inability to take things lightly, his complicated way of dealing with simple issues, his taste for solitude and alienation, his love of anything he didn't understand, the weird feeling of anguish and unreality he felt at nightfall, the sense of menace.

The car gave him resolve, maturity, and insolence. Not to mention the ability to spend most of his time away from home, at the university. Architecture wasn't only a vocation; it was, above all, a means of imposing distance, something that the faculty building itself contributed to: it had been damaged in the Civil War and had only undergone a very modest renovation since it was reopened in the postwar period, thus heightening the impression of existing in another era: a bunker in temporal suspension, accessed by long corridors. A number of white glass globes, resembling plastic footballs, cast a dim light on the bronze busts of provosts whose names, inscribed on small plaques, he could never be bothered to read. When he started his studies, repairs had just begun on the roof of the north wing, where an unexploded shell was discovered in the foundations, and for weeks afterward he read about the clashes that had taken place in the University City.

Starting out on a major he was passionate about didn't distract him from the breach. The day the rusty shell was found, he wanted to send everything flying through the air; he was all too often irritated by the professors, the student cliques, and the ordinary-looking women who drew in charcoal. He liked to take refuge in the west-facing rose garden and gaze toward a horizon broken by Fernando Higueras's beautiful, extraterrestrial "crown of thorns," one of the few examples of Madrid's contemporary architecture that didn't make him want to move to another country. It may be that what prevented that breach with his family from closing was the transformation he saw in Older Brother, whose sole legal guardian he'd become after his mother had washed her hands of her son. His brother's new state of mental health entered his freshman's bloodstream with the force of things both long desired and long feared.

Even before he'd enrolled in the School of Architecture, changes to Older Brother's medication had left him more alert, and they were now close. They'd discuss current affairs, family matters—although the rest of the family rarely visited—friendships with other patients, and even the possibility of leaving the clinic. That closeness, which felt amazing after missing it for so long, merged with Older Brother's delusions, and it was in fact those delusions that lay behind the trips they began to make together. Older Brother was no longer content to see him only on Saturdays, so now he often swung by the clinic after class. His brother was convinced that he could hear the voices of the dead, so they visited all the cemeteries in Madrid because, he said, the connection was purer in those places. They walked in La Almudena, the Civil, the Hebrew and English Cemeteries, in La Florida, the Norte, the Sacramental de San Lorenzo y San Pedro, the Santa María, the San Pedro, and the San Sebastián. There, Older Brother seemed to recover his wits—he was less tongue-tied, the imbecilic look of remote stupefaction disappeared from his eyes—enough to say that he'd gotten the job at the Ministry of Defense because of his powers as a medium and awareness of where conspiracies were being hatched. The excursions from the clinic became more capricious, more eccentric. At his brother's insistence, they made it as far as a large house in the town of Guadarrama, near the La Jarosa reservoir. In the garden they came across a girl who was crying; she told them that her mother was dying. Older Brother remained silent for some time, as if in meditation, then stroked the girl's hair. On another occasion, he demanded to be smuggled out of the clinic late at night and driven to an industrial estate in Vicálvaro, where Older Brother broke into a warehouse. He'd waited in the car, expecting the police to catch his brother stealing some ridiculous piece of junk, but nothing happened. Older Brother refused to offer any explanation and, once again, was abnormally lucid, seemingly without a trace of mental illness. He stopped asking questions in case his brother became suspicious, started thinking that he was one of those censors who had hung a sign around his brother's neck saying "disturbed." For Older Brother, the illness was the world's long, vengeful lack of comprehension. "They are afraid of what I know," he'd say, but sometimes he spoke with shame about his derangement, and was pained to have lost everything. Those moments of intense nostalgia, with their level of normality, were few and far between. What his brother usually displayed was a tangle of overlapping strata and an inability to remember what his life had been like before his illness. He, for his part, attempted to immerse himself in that hodgepodge, to understand rather than discount it, and even to superimpose it on his own, to find fun in it. One day he made a joke about the firebird his brother claimed to see every morning on his bed. Older Brother had laughed, but then looked at him in sullen confusion before running off.

It was during one of those moments of taking liberties with Older Brother's condition that something arose which he'd always suspected deep down, although never in that way, as though he'd been carrying around a toy knife and suddenly found a painful, bleeding wound in his abdomen.

Architecture students had to make drawings of the urban environment. And given that his brother believed the devil presided over the city, it occurred to him to view its buildings from a demoniacal perspective. He noted down outlandish ideas, such as that the façade of Nuestra Señora de Cristo Santo had a stained glass window with circles containing inverted pentagrams, or that in the Pasaje de la Rueca in San Blas there were numerous paintings of Baphomet. One night, while jotting down one of these observations over a beer in a tasca in La Cornisa, he thought he saw his brother entering the Seminario Conciliar. He went to a pay phone and called the clinic. The doctor on duty informed him that his brother wasn't there and reminded him that he himself, as the legal guardian, had decided against their advice that the patient should enjoy a level of independence. He returned to the seminary and climbed the wall, convinced that Older Brother would be in one of the rooms overlooking the garden. At that hour, with the clouds gathering over the Parque de Atenas and the building swathed in a fine mist, the pointed tips of the cypresses had a spectral quality. He sat on the grass for a long time without seeing anything besides light streaming from windows, until the building merged with the shadows and he felt more anxious than ever as the whole city sank into profoundly sinister darkness. The only sound was the immense solitude of nocturnal Madrid, its harshness, its surliness, the empty parks, the bars where no songs were being sung. He was afraid that his brother was watching him, but at some point he fell asleep, had a tough, irascible dream, and woke feeling as if several trains had passed over him. The next day he behaved normally during his visit to his brother, not wanting to interrogate him, although he had the feeling that everything he said was filled with ambiguity.

Every night that week he stood outside the seminary, and just when he was on the point of concluding that he'd been mistaken, he saw Older Brother—his oversized raincoat, slight hunch, and rather clumsy gait—pass through the entrance to the building. Everything he'd thought until that moment was turned upside down and he told himself that the universe of delusions didn't exist only on an imaginary plane. *Something* existed, and illness might be just an excuse, the lid covering the other life his brother lived behind everyone else's backs, perhaps even his own. He climbed the wall and walked among the tulip trees in the garden. Even though he hadn't heard any dogs barking the last time he was here, he imagined a mastiff running out from behind the boxwood hedge. Lying on the lawn, he examined the windows; if a seminarian noticed him, he'd take him for a beggar or a park thief, if such a thing existed. When he got home, at two in the morning, he was overcome by a sense of unreality so profound that he was unable to sleep. He was shivering; his feet refused to warm up even when he rested them on the radiator. The following day he made a date with Emilia, a model with blond locks and ginger pubic hair whom he'd sketched in charcoal. He didn't go to classes, he didn't stand outside the seminary. Instead, he invited Emilia to a hotel and lost his virginity to her almost without noticing—his hard-on only lasted the three seconds it took to penetrate her—and then he slipped into grotesque sullenness. He didn't respond to anything she said; he put his right hand in a sock to make a puppet and repeatedly went to the bathroom to move his bowels without closing the door, as if he wanted Emilia to leave but only had the courage to tell her in this pathetic, inconsiderate way. In fact, he didn't know what he wanted, and Emilia eventually left. He was very close to suffering an attack, and if he managed to get ahold of himself—he'd suspect much later—it was only because he spent almost two weeks in bed with a virus and a fever that produced a momentary repair of one of the letters on the keyboard in his head that had stopped functioning.

When he recovered, he reduced the amount of time he spent with Older Brother, only going with his sister on the regular Saturday visits. Curiosity, however, eventually got the better of him. One morning he played hooky from university and stood outside the clinic. He saw his brother come out at midday with his medicated grin and an unusual air of determination and board a bus. He got off in Hortaleza, where he walked to a makeshift church with an asbestos cement roof. Leaving his car and standing near the church, he heard a cry of relief. It wasn't the sound of a man or a woman, but wasn't a child either. There were three voices coming from inside the ramshackle construction, and one of them was his brother's. As he returned to his car, his legs felt weak, as if he'd been kicking a killer. It occurred to him that Older Brother might be a mentor in some kind of spiritual discipline. The next week, another cry, similar to that previous one, broke the silence of a modest house in the Tetuán neighborhood, and he heard yet another in the hallway of an apartment building he'd managed to sneak into. He'd seen an elderly woman wearing an expression of horror open the door for his brother and make the sign of the cross as if he were a saint. She was crying. Standing on the musty terrazzo stairs, he heard two voices, one of them sounding like it came from a cave, the other belonging to Older Brother. There was a furious argument, the voices were fighting to the death, and then he had no idea what to think because, rather than producing images or words, his body began to shiver uncontrollably. His architecture studies were no help when it came to abandoning his espionage, his obsession; during the final weeks of the semester, the students were expected to spend most of their time either sketching in the street or drawing up plans for various assignments. He attempted to find ways of combining these two activities with his investigation; he imagined himself carrying a visibly huge folder, his fingers red with chilblains, surrounded by curious passersby who'd stopped to ask if he was a professional artist. He had to work with incredible speed to ensure that his drawings met the approval of the School, but when he showed them to his tutor he was told that the sketches didn't meet the guidelines, and that he should focus on a single building in its context.

The Sacramento church came too late to receive a passing grade on any of his assignments: although it allowed him to work in great detail, the fact that he'd failed to put together a team of fellow students to help with drawing up the plans meant that his urbanism project would be reduced to a single street and so could only be submitted for the baroque module of architectural analysis. But it was the one project that allowed him to continue his pursuit of his brother, who by then was visiting the church on a daily basis.

On his first two visits, he walked around the interior and approached the sacristy, which was completely silent. He wandered like a ghost, observing the parishioners, the unfussy Castilian baroque, the fresco at the entrance in which angels with phylacteries like DNA chains stood over a brown figure, something like a blotch or a dust storm. There were tapestries, one depicting a Crucified Christ and another a Virgin, each with the emblem of Christ of the Halbadiers: two halbadiers and a royal crown. They were horrendous.

He suspected that someone had driven Older Brother to this historic place of worship, but the galleries were un-lit and the traffic muffled any other sound. During those first two days he was able to draw without interruption as his brother spent a long time in the building. He made several sketches of the church and the adjoining buildings, made notes for an urbanism study, and generally behaved as though he was going to pass this assignments, despite being sure to fail. He also did research in the library and discovered that the church had originally been constructed for Bernadine nuns, whose former convent had now disappeared without a trace. Apparently, the architect had fallen out of favor and so work hadn't begun on the church until fifty years after its conception. None of the original plans had been preserved, but he noticed one remarkable fact: even though surveying equipment had been used on several occasions to establish the dimensions of the church, the resulting measurements had never tallied, as if the building moved, making it impossible to capture its form. That fact seemed coherent with his brother's life, as did the story of the place being haunted by the ghost of an old man, decapitated by thieves in 1753. The headless old man first appeared shortly after his death to reveal the identity of his executioners.

He toyed with the unlikely hypothesis that Older Brother had become a priest, a crazy exorcist, but never the one wearing vestments or elevating the chalice. He couldn't imagine him hearing confession either. The only change in the routine was that he stayed in the church a little longer each day, leaving at the crack of dawn, which led to the thought that Older Brother had dinner there and that the large granite and presumably sumptuous building abutting the church served food.

One Thursday, sitting in the car, he saw his brother's form behind the lace curtains in one of the rooms. A dry palm leaf hung from the balcony. Older Brother was crossing from one side of the room to the other, and there was something unnatural about his walk, as though he was trying to intimidate someone, or even playing with a football. Then the lights went out. Shivers coursed through his body again; his bones and muscles knew, divined, what his head rationalized, made opaque. The episode was repeated on three consecutive nights, always at the same time, and on the fourth the lantern in the dome of the church was lit and, standing outside, he clearly saw his brother's figure high above. He didn't remember any access to the dome inside the church or a footbridge across to it. The next day, after mass, he asked the parish priest if it was possible to get up to the dome and the lantern. "Only when it's being cleaned, and then the workers need a harness," was the reply. "Well, I've seen a man up there," he insisted, and the priest then asked him to leave. That same night, under a supernaturally black sky without a single star, he again saw someone in the dome. It was Older Brother, standing stock-still, watching him with a fixed expression on his face, showing that his vigil had been going on for hours; suddenly his shadow moved from the dome to the old building and began to pass through the rooms. He was able to catch glimpses of it through the thin, improper, immodest curtains. There was no pause between one room and the next, as if the walls had been demolished. Older Brother reached the chamber with the balcony and palm leaf, and an eerie mist descended over the whole street.

THE TOP FLOOR ROOM

The good news that causes everyone such inexplicable fear.
—CHARLES BAUDELAIRE

The first night she heard a crash so loud she thought someone must be killing a guest in the next room, or using a
jackhammer on the body. Or it could have been a monster
throwing chairs at the ceiling and making holes in the
floor. There was no room adjoining hers, at least that was
what the housekeeper had said. Yet the noise was coming from behind the wall. Added to the monster-machine
racket, she heard two men who seemed to be playing
some kind of game. They were speaking English. It occurred to her that in the bedroom, whose existence the
housekeeper had denied, some very loud, violent sexual
practice involving the furniture and fixtures was being
carried out. For instance, one of the blond men—she
guessed that they were blond because they were speaking English—was undressing and, as he took off each
item, was whacking a baseball bat against the toilet bowl.
The other was wearing boxing gloves; he'd taken down a
picture, hung a shirt in its place, and was punching it. It

was a weird scenario, but it seemed possible to her. She waited until the noise stopped to go out barefoot, wearing just a T-shirt, into the hallway. There was no door there. Besides her room, the only things on that floor were the water heaters and the elevator machinery.

She was living in the hotel where she worked. The pay was bad because her room and full board were deducted from her wages. Two waiters working under the same conditions slept in the basement, next to the laundry. Even though it was smaller, she preferred her bedroom on the top floor because it had a view of the whole city.

She spent the day in the hotel kitchen. Her first task each morning was to scramble the pasteurized eggs served for breakfast and put them in a chafing dish. The congealed yellow mixture was maintained at a constant temperature from seven to half past ten, unless the waiters failed to notice when someone left off the lid. Then the eggs went from hot to warmish. The same happened with the bacon, sausages, and the roast potatoes sprinkled with thyme. These elements of an imperfect English breakfast were scarcely touched. Very few foreigners stayed in the hotel. The majority of the guests came from other Spanish provinces to do business at the fairs held in the building across the street, well known for its corten-steel façade designed by a famous architect who had been the object of furious criticism and no less passionate praise in the local media. The people who shuttled between the hotel dining room and the rusty-looking building preferred the tostadas with olive oil, tomatoes, and ham to the full English, even though the ham was of extremely poor quality.

Did any of the dishes served there taste good? She sometimes felt guilty about the lack of gusto with which the diners ate the swordfish in parsley sauce or the breaded filet. There were two chefs: she was one, the other was a woman in her fifties from Burgos. They were both good cooks, but it was impossible to make a decent salad with iceberg lettuce and tomatoes that looked like the fruit of some nuclear disaster. The canned carrots and beets tasted of acidity regulators. The salchichas were veined with long strips of tough pork. The green vegetables in the mixed salad were always soggy, even though they weren't over-cooked, and the mayonnaise left a sour taste in the mouth. Toxic fat seeped from the longaniza sausage and they had to make the Spanish omelet with roast potatoes left over from breakfast, scraping off the thyme before mixing them with the pasteurized egg and milk. She wasn't even al-lowed to add a splash of olive oil to the pan to brighten up the dish. The fish, which came in large bags, was always dry and there seemed to be no difference between the hake and the cod. The only things she liked preparing for herself were the vegetarian sandwiches, with either hard-boiled or fried egg. When she chose to fry the egg, the yolk would ooze greasily out of the small holes in the bread. She'd gotten into the habit of having a fried egg sandwich for lunch and a hardboiled egg one for dinner almost every day. Except for the lentil soup, which was served once a week, she couldn't stand anything else on the menu. She got through the mornings on orange juice from a carton, and on Wednesdays sighed with pleasure over her bowl of lentil soup. The fact was that she and La Burgos had no option but to follow the recipe book, which stipulated the daily menu and the dishes that were to lie like dead insects in the display cabinet at the bar. La Burgos, who lived in the city with her electrician husband and two children, used to say that they shouldn't complain, since trying to make anything halfway good with those inferior ingredients would just be frustrating.

During the first week she dreamed of pieces of talking food. Frozen artichokes, peas the size of closets, and pallid chicken breasts floated up to her room in the sky. The foods introduced themselves one by one and a multitude of voices spoke through them. Everything was ambiguous, except for the voices, which were deafening. They remained burned into her memory for a long time, and in the mornings, as she chopped garlic for the liver tapas, the prospect of going back to spend another night in that hidey-hole disturbed her. She didn't know why she called it a hidey-hole because it wasn't hidden or a hole. The windows overlooked a wide avenue, and it got so much light that she fantasized she was living in a hot air balloon. No one else ever went up there. Would anyone come to her aid if she had a stroke?

Hidey-hole also made her think of a kidnapping. Had she kidnapped herself? Was she being kidnapped by the food, by those gigantic kernels of sweet corn swollen with water and sorbic acid? She had the feeling that she was. That was why she had those dreams of crab sticks, broad beans, and chorizo in white wine. The chorizo made the floor slippery. Her slippers skated over it; sometimes she went flying, and then she had to throw out the clothes she'd been wearing because the hotel's washing machines were incapable of getting out the reddish, greasy stain. In her dreams, she had no clothes left, and there were many days when she believed she'd lost the ones she'd dreamed about until she found them in a drawer.

The intensity of those dreams was in complete contrast to the innocuousness of her working day. She was an invisible cog in the machinery of the hotel. In addition, she was a bit plain, so the waitresses weren't jealous of her and the male receptionists never came on to her. Her features were so average, so unremarkable, that, on the rare occasions when she left the kitchen, the guests never noticed that a living being was crossing the dining room.

One night she dreamed of a crocodile walking on water that was streaming down walls. The crocodile was in a remote region of Africa. Although with the internet and low-cost flights, nothing was really remote now, in her dream the world was unbounded and mysterious. The images must come from her childhood, she thought. But she immediately discounted that supposition: the place where she'd been raised had been nothing like that humid dream environment with its unidentifiable smell, which was neither pleasant nor unpleasant, just new. Like when she was in Havana, although the smell there had been disgusting. And she wasn't really sure if that remote region of Africa wasn't in fact a remote region of Brazil, but that was just because some thin, unprepossessing Brazilians were staying in the hotel. They all wore white Lacoste polo shirts with tiny crocodile logos.

Late one cold night when a cierzo was blowing she

dreamed of gales and tinny voices shouting. That dry north wind squeezed her muscles and bones, making her joints squeak like chalk on a board, forming eddies in her blood, lifting her up, making her disappear behind a screen of minute droplets of red rain. Her dislocated body and the sounds of the city faded into the manager, who was walking across the lobby in the nude without ever reaching his goal: the front desk. Everyone was looking at him, but at the same time it was as if nothing unusual were happening, even if it would have been a good idea for him to put some clothes on before the Abyssinian delegation arrived.

When she woke she was certain she'd dreamed someone else's dream. Maybe the manager's. She checked and found that he'd stayed overnight in the hotel. What did they have in common? He usually left work at half past eight in the evening. He lived in a housing complex and they often chatted because there were certain groups of sales reps who, given the chance, would empty the chafing dishes before they could prepare more food. He used to warn her and La Burgos before that happened, and always added in some piece of gossip. "Have you heard the latest?" She'd laugh from a sense of duty, but also because the manager was a good guy.

Another night she dreamed of a woman who called a radio station to unburden herself. Her son had just died of cancer. In addition to the host, the program had a chorus, who made light of the tragedy. The woman wanted the chorus to forgive her, and there was a perverse link between allowing herself to be humiliated and being pardoned. She was disturbed by how neatly it all fitted together, so different to the usual logic of dreams. When she woke, she wrote down the scene as though it were a play.

In the past she'd enjoyed writing, particularly poetry. At the age of sixteen she'd shown her poems to a girlfriend, who talked about the strength of the images. One day a mutual acquaintance told her that, behind her back, her friend was saying her poetry was really bad but that she was too embarrassed to tell her so. After that, she stopped writing. She didn't see it as giving something up and wasn't angry with her friend. Before the poetry she'd had a thing about drawing blue perfume bottles on wooden panels and writing "In Hawaii" on the labels. She'd also bought herself an electronic keyboard and started practicing the skills she'd learned in her childhood piano classes.

She'd eventually given up on the keyboard, and anything else that she might have excelled in. She hated any form of distinction, particularly after studying fine arts for a year and sharing an apartment in Malaga with an actor. During that time she thought people looked down on her because of her social background—she was the only student who had to work her way through college—and lack of ambition. She dropped out of the fine arts class, returned home to her mother in Huesca, and took a course in hotel management. Being broke began to seem like a virtue. Her mother was upset; she'd always wanted her two daughters to make something of themselves. That was why she'd sent them to the conservatory. Her sister had given up the piano first, and was now a stylist in a Marco Aldany salon.

She didn't like the scene she'd written about the woman calling a radio station. It felt gross. But she didn't destroy it. She was aware of something too vivid, not in the images themselves, but in the way the dream had unfolded, something she could access through her text. At lunch she heard a customer tell La Burgos that her eldest child had died of stomach cancer and she was doing everything in her power to die in the same way. The third time the customer had asked for her steak to be cooked longer, La Burgos had come out of the kitchen to check on why anyone would order charred meat before she went ahead and ruined it. Charred meat, the customer explained, was carcinogenic. She'd started drinking, smoking, and eating burned meat so that her body would develop malignant cells. When La Burgos spluttered a "But, señora…" the customer replied:

"Forget the 'but señora'! I'm not bothering anyone. I just want my meat to be charred. That's what I'm paying for."

The woman was either out of her mind or trying to cause a scene, or maybe both. That was when she was certain that in addition to dreaming the manager's dream, she'd dreamed that woman's. She also knew that even the nightmares with giant baby carrots and other foodstuffs were not based on her personal experiences but those of some rep staying there during a trade fair whose expense account didn't stretch beyond the unexceptional hotel dining room. She imagined a bald man with round eyes, approaching retirement age. She imagined him as deeply embittered, with bushy, arched eyebrows that disguised the pained expression on his face. She imagined that the rancid mushroom reminded him of his dried-out relationship with his wife: they both took away his appetite and put him in a bad mood.

Her dreams expanded. A single night would include several different guests, and in the mornings she'd try to work out which of them were the shadows that had stationed themselves at her bedside…which was the middle-aged woman from Andalusia who'd promised to be back in a moment but then disappeared, giving rise to a sexy chase scene involving the presumably male dreamer. She wasn't always sure about their gender, as if it made no difference to those unconscious minds. And she was never certain whether, for example, the children were the sons, granddaughters, cousins, or even siblings of the sleepers. Sometimes it was all quite boring, nothing more than reproductions of humdrum days: the bustle of the toy fair with a backdrop of dancing dolls; a car trip with a stop at a Monegros rest area; hurried attempts to pack a suitcase that was constantly changing shape.

Trying to sort out whose dreams were whose was exhausting. She knew both a lot and nothing at all about the dreamers. If she came across the man who night after night dreamed about a woman, possibly his mother, who was always humiliating him, all she'd discover about him was some everyday conflict. What these people were hiding, and what she herself was hiding from others, were ordinary problems, and only the fact of not speaking about a common ailment, or taking it too seriously, made it an anomaly.

One day she saw herself in a dream. She didn't enjoy the experience. It seemed to involve a mad dog that might tear her to pieces. Her own image was breaking up. Her hips contracted or her legs shrunk; tiny black wrinkles were covering her face like the footprints of flies; she was wearing a low-cut top from which bulged heavy breasts that dragged down her shoulders. She was certain that the person dreaming her was male due to something she called sibilance. It wasn't that the sibilance had anything to do with the person's breathing, the word just fit her impression of being recreated by a man. One night that man appeared as a baker from Teruel who invited her to accompany him to a coastal town. He was wearing a white apron and a paper hat, and he had a kiln at the shore that functioned as a brick factory. He drove her to a house with no electricity or running water, and tried to pretend that it was a hotel. He'd be staying there too. She felt the man's expectations being dashed in advance. It was impossible to say anything about her own feelings. In that dream she was simply a cold body, a few years older than her present age, with a head of curly hair. When she woke, she had a slight sense of apprehension. Whoever was dreaming her, she didn't find him in the least attractive.

That man's dreams became more frequent. He wasn't always a baker, sometimes he appeared as an old man who hid her away in his home, or in others as a surgeon wearing a suit and tie, carrying a briefcase. She tried to investigate the guests from the tourist industry who regularly stayed in the hotel. Although they were in an economic crisis, the city had had a stroke of luck. A branch of a famous modern art museum was about to open and it was predicted that the number of tourists would triple in the coming years.

Her main means of spying on the clients was a peep-hole in the kitchen. Occasionally she'd take trays of hard melon or slices of cheese to the breakfast buffet. A great many people attended the trade fairs, there was a lot of noise and bustle; the singles who occupied tables near the door or either side of the large window were masks, focused on buttering their croissants, replying to WhatsApp messages, or leafing through the local newspaper.

She worked from seven in the morning to eleven at night, with a three-hour break after lunch, and for that whole time she wore a tight white cap that left her hair dull and flattened to her scalp. During her break, she either went up to her room to sleep or out onto the street. She particularly liked to be outdoors when there was a cierzo blowing; there were no other pedestrians to be seen, only cars, and since the stores were closed until half past five, people stayed inside for fear of being hit by the awnings flying crazily in the wind. She found calm in the empty squares, the sound of the cierzo, the sense of being a dancing nocturnal animal. She walked with her hair loose, and that gusting wind was the only thing capable of returning to her locks the vigor that had been stolen by her cap. It gave her hair a ruffled, anarchic gloss, with tangled knots that she combed out after taking a scalding hot shower to wash away the cold.

She saved almost all her salary. There was nothing she needed to spend it on. By the time her days off came around she was worn out; instead of the usual two free days a week, she had to work four weeks without a break and then take eight days' leave, which did have its advantages.

There was something mystical about her weariness, her habit of sometimes surviving on only orange juice until late into the evening—when she'd treat herself to a fried egg sandwich—or walking in the cierzo, chasing the image of an unreal city. In fact, she was far from understanding what she was feeling. Perhaps it was some sick form of satisfaction. When her free days came around, she'd return to Huesca to stay with her mother and sister; their chatter, the ribs and potato stew, and the after-dinner hours in front of the TV were all comforting. Plus she didn't dream. She began to think that her room in the hotel held some magical power that enabled the dreamscapes to ascend the stairs to invade her head, and that as soon as she quit her job everything would return to normal.

Summer was not far off. The cierzo blew up less frequently, but the sun was so fierce that it left the city as dry and impotent as the wind had. Then she started to dream La Burgos's dreams and her feelings went beyond weariness or disgust, even though she herself didn't even appear in her colleague's nocturnal adventures. La Burgos's hands and forearms were always covered in flour. She had to serve glasses of cava without getting them floury. White lumps fell from her skin as she carried the tray into the dining room; once there, she'd realize that her index finger and thumb were untouched by the flour, which meant she wouldn't leave marks on the glasses. Unfortunately, she'd accidentally make some movement that dusted those digits too. She'd decide to trust in miracles. She'd pick up the glasses with her whitened hands, hoping that the flour wouldn't cling to the surface. Obviously, they got all smudged with floury fingerprints, but La Burgos wasn't going to be beaten. There still remained the possibility that the diners wouldn't notice. Those elegantly dressed people weren't looking at her flour-dusted forearms, as if a chef spent her days making nothing but pizza dough. Their lack of attention increased her hope that the flour wouldn't be noticed, would be taken as some natural attribute of the glasses, or marks thoughtfully made by the head waiter so they would know where to position their fingers when the toast was made, thus avoiding an awkward breach of etiquette.

She felt that in the dreams La Burgos was laying the blame on her, even sometimes in her absence, and that she was becoming the target of her colleague's uncontrollable rage. She didn't believe that there was any meaning in the dream world, but she didn't believe that there wasn't either. Maybe La Burgos only hated her in her sleep. But what if that wasn't true? This uncertainty troubled her because she trusted her colleague. She never told her much about herself and would have been too embarrassed to recount her walks in the cierzo. And, despite her nonstop chatter, La Burgos didn't have much to say about herself either. Her prattle was like the flapping of a small bird: it flew almost invisibly through the air. She heard it as a soft whistling, and the sound shielded her. Although she wasn't quite sure from what. Perhaps from the morning receptionist, who used to have breakfast with them, making jokes about the housekeeper's ass, her voice, the way she dyed her hair: it was so black that in the LED-lit lobby it emitted a piercing blue sheen. They thought that if the receptionist badmouthed the housekeeper, she probably did the same to them behind their backs.

There was something else that worried her: she could no longer be sure that the dreams were rising from the rooms below; it seemed possible that they came from any-where at all. If what was happening to her was unrelated to the hotel and her room in the sky, she might never stop dreaming other people's dreams. That thought led to others, until she finally went out into the street to walk aimlessly. The avenues were like her head when she was asleep, when her mental processes were besieged by invading beings. She couldn't say which streets she'd chosen to walk down and which had chosen her. When she got to the hotel, she had no idea if she'd consciously made her way there or if her arrival was a matter of chance. And she didn't know how long she'd been walking. The assistant manager was waiting for her with his arms folded across his chest. She gazed at her reflection in the mirror, searching for some clue in her hair, the blackened hem of her shirt, the slender blade of grass right in the center of her chest. Perhaps she'd spent days wandering in the open air and her face was aglow. Her cheeks might be smudged with dirt and her arms purple with bruises. What she saw in the mirror was a very pale complexion, hair like steel wool, as though she'd been walk-ing face first into a cierzo of incredible strength. The color had fled from her skin, it was almost transparent; three but-tons were missing from her shirt and her jeans looked like they had been trampled into the dance floor of a nightclub. She didn't remember any cierzo. In fact, she didn't remem-ber anything. She felt hungry and faint.

"Do that once more and you're out," said the assistant manager. "You're only getting away with it this time because there's no fair and Trini managed on her own. How did you get in such a state?"

She wanted to say something: apologize, promise that it wouldn't happen again, tell the assistant manager that she'd gotten lost, and with the stress and the hunger, had fainted in the street. That would justify her appearance and her amnesia. But no words came to her lips. She was overcome by a fear that her voice would break, that some interminably long pitiful wail would issue from her mouth if she attempted to speak. The grubby white curtains in the office gave a glimpse of the silent darkness outside. The assistant manager worked late when the books had to be balanced. Was this one of those days? Or perhaps it was now winter, which would explain the early darkness: that idea seemed outlandish, although in her head anything felt possible. But if she'd been wandering around the city for months, the assistant manager wouldn't even have recognized her. She touched her bare arm, the hairs like a hen's down. The assistant manager had let her go without commenting on her silence. Did she speak so rarely that it caused no surprise?

When she plugged in her phone to charge it, the clock showed 12:43 a.m., one day ahead. She'd missed a whole shift. On her return to the kitchen, La Burgos didn't complain about her absence, and she thought that maybe she'd forgotten about it. The days were all so similar that they erased memory. Then her thoughts grew darker. Was she losing her mind? She dreamed that La Burgos was inside a car, parked on a bleak plateau. The sun was high in the sky and its light was blinding, but rather than warming the air, the chill it spread across the earth was so intense it made La Burgos squirm like a small, newborn creature facing death. She could taste her colleague's hatred of her; despite the fact that she formed no part of the life of that dream being, she came to the conclusion that the level of ill will displayed by those dream contortions must correspond to something real. And she couldn't bear that. Since she still had to prove that there was a relationship between living in the hotel and dreaming other people's dreams, she began to spend certain nights outdoors. It was the end of July when she made the decision to distance herself from those dreams.

The summer nights made these escapades easier. The first time, she was scared that someone might mug her so she chose a bench downtown. It was a Saturday; she was surrounded by people walking from one bar to the next. Two girls approached her to ask if she was all right. With so much noise, it was 4 a.m. before she managed to fall into a light sleep: not deep enough to determine if her dream was or wasn't her own. Four days later she left the hotel quietly and again stayed downtown. Although there weren't as many partiers, she didn't choose either the main street or the square, but opted instead for the Ensanche area, stretching out on a stone bench by a planter. Before settling in for the night, she took a quick look inside the pub across the street; there were couples and single men, most likely alcoholics. A potpourri of 90s Spanish music issued from the premises: bland, tense, cracked sounds.

That night she dreamed of a water trough in which she submerged her recently shaved legs. The redness of the pores and a deep-seated warmth cooled in waves, and something critical resolved itself. She woke just before the alarm on her phone sounded and cheerfully got up from the bench, a piece of bird shit on her cardigan. Her feet were frozen; the below zero night still hovered in the air. But by nine that morning, when she was replenishing the trays of ham and cheese, she was in a sweat. The sun was beating down on the bare sidewall of the building and the air conditioner had broken down.

After months of being dispossessed of a part of her life, and with its recuperation now in sight, she nevertheless found it hard to come to terms with the loss of her own personal dreams. One Tuesday, sometime after midnight, she got up and, without changing her nightshirt—it was red and looked like a dress—went out into the street. This time she opted for a row of benches near a church. That secluded place showed its age in a way that was different from the downtown buildings, with their tawdry, short-lived ornamentation. She fell asleep the minute she lay her head down and didn't open her eyes until dawn. She had the impression that the city was empty. The streets were silent and the fresh, early morning air, which would soon disappear in the blazing sun, seemed to belong on some astral plane rather than in the earth's atmosphere. She got to her feet. A police siren cut through the air. It was a dense sound, twitchy, as if jumping between various forms of deafening melodies. The silence had ended. Shutters grated as they were opened, the traffic roared; the city was waking and stretching. She ran back to the hotel but still arrived late. The receptionist gave her a silly, suggestive look and said, "What a cute dress." She didn't respond. When she got to her room, she put on her uniform and, without even washing her face, went to the kitchen. La Burgos's dreams hadn't invaded her sleep. To be honest, she didn't remember what she'd dreamed, although the emptiness around her when she woke, as if the city had become an architect's model, did belong to some forgotten personal dream sequence.

The next time, she was better equipped. She bought a used camping mat and a light blanket to protect her from the cool of the early morning and from any passing low-lifes, who, if she were well covered, would take her for a panhandler and not rob her. And her skinny, angular body was no temptation; with that blanket over her she was unlikely to arouse sexual desire. She could spend the night near the river or in a park, places she guessed would be more comfortable and allow for deeper sleep, for a more complete conquest of her dreams. She hadn't counted on the swarms of mosquitos on the riverbank that buzzed around her ears the whole night, even when she'd pulled the blanket over her head. That riot of winged creatures seeking her blood prevented her from resting. She returned to the hotel covered in bites; the one on her eyelid swelled up like a football until a chambermaid applied some cream from the first-aid box. She changed her mind about sleeping in parks or by the river after that, and took refuge beneath a newly constructed bridge over an esplanade that had formerly been a shantytown. The beautiful, white bridge connected the railway station with the already famous modern art gallery that was to be opened in six months, and the esplanade was only used by kids from the adjoining buildings, who played ball games or lay on their backs watching the planes pass overhead. But there was also a grand plan for the redevelopment of the area, or that's what people said. It took her over an hour to get there, and when she was under one of the pilings of the bridge, with the strong smell of piss, she felt that she had too much city at her back. The gigantic concrete circle of the esplanade surrounded by apartment buildings reminded her of her room at the hotel: it was a state of exception, a territory that was tearing itself off from any rational space. She dreaded to think what might happen in that huge expanse. Would she be invaded by the dreams of thousands of people? Would that multitude in her head shatter her? Her first supposition was correct. Having moved away from the pilings and the smell of piss, she did receive simultaneous dream fragments, which she watched as if she possessed the gift of ubiquity. Although she didn't wake in thousands of pieces, she noted that her mind now knew much more than she did: she was only able to recall scraps of that knowledge. In some part of her, all those dreams were still reproducing themselves. Instead of being destroyed by this invasion, she felt calm, and had the sense that the esplanade was no larger than her home in Huesca. She remembered a poem in which a crowd of people go out into the street. The time had come for action, for going to work, for dressing for mourning. She could only recall a snatch of it:

> For the last hour, for exactly the last hour
> a million people have been about to leave their homes.
> For the last hour, since half past seven this morning,
> a million people have been about to leave their homes.

She'd noted down those lines years ago, while they were being recited by a host on Radio 3 during a program on urban poetry. She was surprised that the presenter hadn't chosen anything involving Huesca. After all, Huesca is a city, she told herself. That's when she started writing down the poems. When she took the job at the hotel, it seemed as if the view from her window was indeed present in those lines. A million people left their homes every morning at a particular time. And at that moment, under the white bridge, with the esplanade like a long tongue stretching out into infinity, she was absolutely certain that the number of people going to their offices or construction sites was much larger. There were so many that if you added them up, the figure would be astronomical. It was time to go back to work, but she was incapable of taking her eyes off the distant people, on the balconies of condos and in the street. She was also waiting for someone to cross the esplanade. Time passed, but the expanse of concrete remained empty, as though the inhabitants of the nearby apartments avoided setting foot in it. Not even the people walking their dogs strayed from the narrow stretch of yellowing grass along the perimeter. She knew she'd be unable to leave until someone crossed the center of the circle.

A boy, who in the distance looked as tiny as a fingertip, approached the edge and stood gazing at her for a long time. Maybe he was trying to work out if she was a person or a doll. There were missed calls from the assistant manager on her phone. She was fired, the messages said, but the word "fired" didn't sound like she was being thrown out; for her it was more like she was launching herself over all those streets where the inhabitants had dreams that would assault her the moment she closed her eyes. For an instant she longed for her room in the hotel, the clean towels, her morning shower, the placid hatred of La Burgos, her own dispossession, against which she was now rebelling in favor of something she couldn't quite get ahold of. The boy took a few steps closer and stopped again. Then he took a few more. She wondered if the child's wariness had to do with her or the esplanade. The locals had probably wanted a park rather than this barren patch of concrete, and now they and their children were boycotting it. Or perhaps they weren't used to seeing homeless under the bridge, and a whispered rumor had been spreading through the buildings since first light: there's a crazy woman sleeping down there. The child continued to approach, but before he got near enough to get a good look at her, she got to her feet and left.

MEMORIAL

She received an alert. A portion of a black-and-white photograph. A thin nose, a cheek. An ear with a familiar shape. It wasn't the whole face, but that didn't stop her food from coming back up three times. Those bitter gastric juices were also due to the nickname: Apep Otein.

She'd never liked pseudonyms, yet that didn't explain her distress. A sense of foreboding forced her to wait five days before opening the Facebook app on her phone. That was when her anxiety turned into terror. What she saw was the face of her mother, who had died two weeks before. Then she noticed that the name was her mother's written backward. Apep Otein = Pepa Nieto.

The photograph was from the seventies, and she would have bet anything that it had never left the living room shelf. Yet it didn't seem likely that her father, the only other person who had access to the family albums, would have opened a Facebook account with a portrait of his wife at the age of twenty-seven and her name written in reverse. Unless he was going mad.

She watched him carefully for a few days. His grief seemed normal. Restrained sorrow, a feeling of abandonment, confusion when he didn't find his wife in the rooms where she was usually to be found doing chores; his senses hadn't yet assimilated the change. She was sure that he wasn't responsible for that misdeed.

Apep Otein had no friends. The home page contained only the photo of Pepa Nieto and a blank wall. Perhaps, she thought, she was the only person who had received a friend request. She didn't accept it, but she didn't block it either. The itch to find out who was behind this macabre initiative and the authority of her mother's image, her name written backward, won out over common sense.

She'd restricted access to her account since the girlfriend of a former lover had started trolling her. During the months before she discovered the identity of the troll—who presented herself as a man on social media—she developed a phobia of being attacked in the street. When someone told her that the person posting was mentally ill she laughed at herself and her fears. Particularly her fears.

Finding herself using the word "trolling" again was a shock, as if it were a self-fulfilling prophecy. She'd been overly hasty in deciding that fear could be disdained, and was now afraid that there were higher powers ready to punish that lack of caution.

She waited for the message that would confirm that Apep Otein's profile masked some warped person who had the means to enter her house and search through the albums until the photo was found.

And it wasn't just any old photo, but her favorite among the hundreds of images of Pepa Nieto. When she was a child, she'd spent hours gazing adoringly at that snapshot, as if everything that was her mother had been present on that day in 1975, before her daughter's birth. The outcome of those whole evenings of mesmerized gazing was foreseeing a future in which, by force of having looked so carefully at the photo, she could resemble her mother at twenty-seven, could possess the same features, the same sweetness of her beauty, so far removed from her own (she'd inherited her father's plump ungainliness). Until she was in fifth grade her only wish was to be the woman in that portrait.

Puberty broke the spell and her enchantment metamorphosed into resentment. Her desire not to see herself in the maternal mirror dominated all else. During the last months of Pepa's illness she requested a sabbatical to do research at a foreign university. That innocent activity sheltered her from the organ failure, the oxygen tanks, her mother's brutally fleshless body.

The feared message studded with threats never arrived. Apep Otein still had no friends and the wall was empty. It was as if the account had no other purpose beyond its mere existence.

She weighed some kindlier hypotheses. Perhaps her aunt Loli, who liked to commemorate the dead in rather eccentric ways, was the author of the heresy. Her aunt might in fact possess a copy of the photograph, although that supposition didn't really hold water, because it wasn't in Loli's nature not to tell her what she was doing.

As the months went by she landed on the page less and less often and eventually put the whole matter at the back of her mind. Then she visited it again. It was as solitary as ever. The wall was blank, not a single friend. As cold as her dead mother. She decided to accept the friend request.

She tapped the photo, the face in the profile and on the biography. Then, underneath the picture, she noticed the exact date and time when it had been uploaded: July 7, 2001, at six in the morning—the date and time when Pepa Nieto had died in front of her grandmother and godmother. She herself had been asleep on a couch near the deathbed, and they hadn't woken her until the nurse had been informed so that the body could be transferred to the morgue.

That night, while her mother was dying—it was a Thursday and her breathing had been extremely irregular since the Monday—she'd stretched out on the couch, completely exhausted, and her godmother had draped a sheet over her. The way the fabric was lovingly tucked around her shoulders felt identical to when her mother had leaned over her bed to pull up the blankets. It was the last time she felt that bird-like delicacy on her body. She'd slept for a while, until her godmother woke her to say that Pepa had passed away. She knew instantly it had been her mother, through her godmother, who had gently covered her with that sheet; she knew that it was a farewell gesture, a final protective act.

She checked Facebook help to see if it was possible to make changes to the date and time of a post. The answer was alarming: that data could not be modified. The following two nights she scarcely slept, and eventually decided to tell her father. He was lounging in front of the television, and just shrugged his shoulders, as if it were perfectly normal for someone to open an account at the moment of his wife's death with her photo and her name written backward.

Her father's insouciance made things worse. She checked the date and time on Apep Otein's page over and over again, and within a week that act had become an obsession. She clicked on the image every five minutes, anxious to find a mistake, as if her life depended on it. She was playing Russian roulette. This ended with a panic attack so severe that she had to be hospitalized and injected with a tranquilizer. Her short chubby father looked on in despair, as though after losing his wife he now had to witness his daughter's death. She couldn't tell him that her collapse had been caused by the Facebook page. Nor did she mention it to the psychiatrist who visited her, nor to the psychologist. She felt a mixture of rage and shame whenever she spoke to them.

She was prescribed a drug that had effects similar to those of ecstasy. It wasn't the best means of halting her fixation with Apep Otein's profile. In a state of euphoria she became convinced that her daily pilgrimage had nothing to do with checking the date and time of the photograph, but was a way of demonstrating to herself that she was capable of bearing what she saw.

She sought a new explanation. A few rather convoluted but not wholly improbable ideas occurred to her, in all of which chance played a role. For instance, she imagined an identity thief breaking into the house and scanning that snapshot to fatten the list of people whose lives he could impersonate on social media platforms. That atypical burglar selected the best, most beautiful, and happiest photos, the objects of greatest sentimental value in order to lay his trail in virtual space. To be effective, these clues had to be directed only at the people closest to the victim. Another possibility was some family friend who had been in love with her mother and who, when he heard that she was dying in the hospital, had opened that account in a fit of pain, anger, confusion, or simple fear of death, with the sinister coincidence that the post was made at the moment his beloved passed away. She told herself that the person must have been asking for her friendship but then, when the period of mourning had passed, felt embarrassed about it or had forgotten his rash act. She also told herself that, under the effects of her medication, those suppositions functioned in the same way as the narcotics, and that she fabricated them as part of the process of reestablishing a form of normalcy that requires an answer to everything.

The pills didn't stop her from going to pieces again on July 7, the anniversary of her mother's death. She opened Facebook as soon as she got up (that morning she and her father were planning to visit the cemetery to put flowers on Pepa's grave) and found Apep Otein's first and so far only post: a photograph of a swimming pool. She immediately recognized the sinuous figure-of-eight form, the indigo paint, the whitewashed wall and chainlink fence.

It was the pool from which she used to look down over

the Cordovan countryside, and was located in the garden of the house where she'd lived until the age of seven, in a village bisected by a national highway. The photo showed still water, no people. The colors were those of the polaroids her parents used to mount in the family albums, but she didn't remember having seen one with only the swimming pool.

The image carried her back to a late afternoon, just before dark, when she and her mother were in the water, its warmth on her body contrasting with the cool air. Pepa had made cheese sandwiches and they ate them in the water, slowly moving their legs. Afterward they lay on the lip of the pool, where the ground still retained the heat of the spring sun, and listened to the vehicles passing on the highway. They played at guessing if they were big or small cars, trucks, or trailers.

She was certain that the first photo on Apep Otein's wall was taken that day when she and her mother watched the sun go down, their swimsuits wet, breathing the pervasive blue smell of chlorine. But that certainty seemed erroneous. Her father had always been the family photographer, and that afternoon he'd been away on business, which explained that unforgettable, extraordinary circumstance: she and her mother alone, with nothing to do except be together.

Before leaving for the cemetery, she checked the albums and boxes and asked her father if he remembered a polaroid of the swimming pool in the house in the country. Even as she spoke, she felt stupid. He never clicked his shutter unless he had people in the frame.

"Maybe it was your mother. I don't remember taking it. Why do you want to know?" he asked.

Her father was getting over the loss of his wife by then. He'd started internet dating. None of the relationships lasted more than two or three weeks, but that didn't bother him. Wouldn't insisting that someone was usurping Pepa's identity by means of images that had never been outside the apartment cast a shadow on his newly found single-status happiness? She didn't mention it again.

It was twelve o'clock when they passed through the gates of the cemetery. They had chosen a somber stone, with a cross so discreetly carved that it was scarcely visible. That austerity contrasted with the heavy bronze crucifixes and relief inscriptions of the other tombs. The burning noon sun conferred upon the graves and that consecrated ground—empty in the stifling heat—a reality that silenced anything not springing from pure stone. The thought of ghosts or lunatics bringing the dead back to life in a virtual space was an impossibility in that place where there was nothing but graves housing bones and her father's pain. A pain that was beginning to owe more to age than anything else.

"Have you arranged to see Luisa today?" she asked.

Luisa was the woman he was currently dating.

"Not today," he answered.

Then he laid a hand on his wife's gravestone, adorned with lilies from the best florist in the city. They would wilt by nightfall.

She went back to compulsively visiting Apep Otein's page, which was eerily silent. There were still no other contacts. She doubled her dose of antidepressants and for forty-eight hours the surge of fluoxetine into her bloodstream left her either laughing out loud at nothing or listlessly gazing at the photo of the swimming pool. When her state stabilized, a new image appeared on the page.

It was her mother, lying on a stretcher next to an ambulance. Her father was holding her hand. The image, a bird's-eye view, encompassed the street, the vehicle, the paramedics and Pepa Nieto, who, barely able to breathe, had decided that evening to have herself admitted to the hospital where she would die. She remembered the scene, not from having seen it before in a photograph, but because she was the person observing it from the living room window. "My final journey," her father later told her Pepa said on the way to the hospital. Her mother had looked up at her for a moment and made a brief gesture in which there was neither pain nor fear because both of those needed strength, and Pepa was exhausted.

It wasn't beyond the bounds of possibility that the photo had been taken by a neighbor. However, the residents of the two apartments above were elderly married couples who didn't seem like they would ever do that sort of thing. And even if the neighbors had been given to eccentric pastimes, she was certain that the image came from her own mind. The view was from the living room window. And what was frozen in the snapshot was her mother's gestured confirmation that she had seen her at the window.

At that moment she knew that there were no limits to what might appear on Apep Otein's wall. And she was right. Two audio files were uploaded; in the first her mother was singing, in the other she was giggling at *Tootsie*, one of her favorite movies. Then came photographs of the restaurants she used to frequent, hotel rooms she'd stayed in, rooms of the houses where she'd lived, the French patisserie she dropped into regularly for coffee and cake, quotations written in notebooks, clothes in shop windows, dishes she'd cooked. They were all related to situations her mother had lived through with her; or rather, that she had lived through with her mother. Those voices and images were scraps of her memory. No one had ever wasted film on a steaming hotpot on the pink and white striped tablecloth that was put out for everyday meals, or shop windows, or dentists' waiting rooms. That archive of memories only existed inside her head. A couple of them did turn up in her photos stored on old cellphones: one was taken after an argument with Pepa in a VIPS restaurant, another in the funeral parlor. In the latter, her mother was laid out for burial, her body on display beneath the glass of the coffin. The shroud couldn't disguise the meagerness of her flesh, and her face was expressionless, there wasn't even a crumb of her past, a glimmer of how death had come to her. Her lips were sealed with adhesive. She'd taken the photo at the instigation of an aunt, who had told her she should have an image of her deceased mother.

"Otherwise you'll regret it," the aunt had insisted.

Although she'd been unwilling to take the photograph, she was superstitious. And she'd always attributed that aunt with a special, indefinable form of wisdom. She'd framed the corpse in the camera on her phone and clicked.

Afterward she looked at the image again and again without the least emotion whatsoever, and not the faintest idea why it might have some value for her in the future. Then she was given a smartphone and the photo was left there, saved on the old one.

On more than one occasion she'd searched for her dead relatives on the internet; often for a cousin who had passed on at twenty-nine. He'd been a security software designer and traces of him could still be found on IT forums. She used to read the responses to technical questions and imagine that behind their professional tact was her cousin, whose name spoken by familiar voices carried her back to all the summer vacations they had spent together. She'd show up at his house when the adults were still taking their siestas and they would go cycling through the white streets of the town. She also searched for earlier generations. She typed her great grandfather's full name into the search engine, or those of the great uncles who had been killed in the war, in the hope of finding some lost information, some mention in an old archive. Naturally, there was nothing, and that void left her speechless, as if the internet had an obligation to contain everything, to alleviate her nostalgia and her thirst for facts. Not long after her mother's death she did a Google search to discover what was left of Pepa Nieto besides her clothes in the closets, her shoes, her books, her cosmetics, and her toothbrush in a glass. The answer was practically nothing: her name on the webpage of the College of Physicians; the flyer for a talk she'd given in Jaén; an official communication announcing her appointment as a pediatrician;

and one other post related to her move to Cordoba.

Apep Otein uploaded a new audio file. It was a violent argument between her mother and father that she had witnessed. She recognized it by the final section: her mother screaming, "Take your hands off me, you son of a bitch!" The slamming of a door that was followed by more shouting and banging. Her father locking Pepa in one of the bedrooms. She heard the child she had been crying, and saw her being locked in another room. In the dark.

Unlike her mother, who could have given master classes in holding grudges, her father was a kindly, fair, calm person. In her memory, that argument was an anomaly. Hearing her childish voice wailing sent a cold shiver down her spine. She told herself that Apep Otein was acting just as her mother would have done in life, seeking out the most painful spots from some vague need that could never be satisfied. She felt pity for her. The following days eased her torment as light-hearted, happy, everyday images returned to the wall. Those suspiciously saccharine scenes made her think that what her mother hoped to achieve through the Facebook account was to invalidate her daughter's memory, leaving only those recollections in which Pepa Nieto played a role, with the result that her past would be completely filled by her progenitor, excluding all experiences in which that woman was not present. As if her life had only involved episodes to which her mother had been a witness.

That notion disturbed her so much that she decided to delete Apep Otein from her life forever. She kept it up for three weeks before finally giving in. When she next passed the cursor over the name, her hand was trembling with impatience. There was no new content on the page. She clicked on the photograph of her dead mother: the face outlined by the shroud, the dark wood of the coffin, the wreaths.

During the period in which she'd abstained from visiting the ghostly wall she'd experienced a disturbing sense of longing. The jumble of images and audio files had been upsetting, so she was surprised to find herself hoping for a fresh memory of Pepa Nieto that had, until now, been buried in her hippocampus, the echo of an ordinary day in her childhood or adolescence: her mother spreading bitter orange marmalade on her bread, cleaning her red ballet slippers, walking her to the bus stop; the outdated idioms used by the whole family when they met up in the spring, and her mother's singing would rise above the chattering voices. Each post had been like discovering a box of dearly loved but mislaid objects that still vibrated with energy.

The strong yearning she'd felt during the time she'd banned herself from visiting the page was no different than what she'd experienced as a child when, after school, she'd have an overwhelming desire to see her mother the moment she got home, only to find her bedroom door locked. Her mother would be doing her hair or makeup, and that terrified her. She'd be unable to stop herself shouting, "Mom, Mom, Mom!" knowing that the door might not be opened. Banishing Apep Otein was like standing on the wrong side of that locked door. She returned to the damned account, clicked on the wall, hesitated for a few seconds and then wrote, screamed:

"Mom!"

What followed was silence and her own emotional response. She cried for that absence, not taking her eyes from the screen, anxiously hoping for her mother to appear. When she recovered from that momentary lapse, the lack of response from the page generated hatred and shock.

For a few weeks there wasn't a single new post. It was as if the page had fulfilled its purpose. Then one evening a long message appeared; a story that Pepa had written for a Cancer Society competition after her first operation. She'd kept that story, along with a silver paperweight in the form of a lizard, a gemstone ring and brooch inherited from her great grandmother, the only things of any value belonging to her mother that hadn't been shared among her aunts. She began reading the story with the impression that her own bewilderment was merging with her mother's.

I didn't know what had happened to me or why I was there. All I could see were tubes.

The first thing I heard was a voice. Was it a man's or a woman's? It was asking me to move both my legs and raise them. I couldn't lift the right one, and I carefully put my hand beneath the sheet to try to work out why. I touched a bandage that came up to my abdomen. There was nothing on the left leg. I vaguely wondered about the cause of that difference, if I'd been left paralyzed. I'd undergone surgery, but couldn't remember anything about it. I don't know how much time passed. I was often able to move my right leg and one day I noticed that the bandage had disappeared.

I made a supreme effort to take in my surroundings. I was still immobilized, hooked up to so many machines I thought I must be about to die. That seemed to be for the best; so much suffering wasn't worth the effort. I went back over my life, feeling very strange. It was like a dream rather than anything real, and I was also very calm, which must have been due to the tranquilizers. Although I found it hard to think clearly, I did realize that there were more serious cases in the unit. Very close to me someone was fighting for breath. Coughing continuously. I had no consciousness of time. That same night or the next one—I figured it was night because of the dim light in the ward, and the dark outside; plus there were no sounds of people coming and going—another patient arrived, screaming all over the place because he couldn't urinate. That really is painful. They gave him all sorts of medication, but he only quieted down for a few minutes at a time.

I was very surprised that none of this bothered me. In fact, I was curious to know what else was going on.

One morning I saw two women standing beside someone lying on another bed. I guessed this person was dying, although that's not what caught my attention: the two women had their eyes fixed on me. They stared at me the whole time they were there, scrutinizing me so hard that I thought their eyeballs might pop. They were probably trying to figure out who I was and couldn't because of all the equipment around my bed.

The colors in the unit changed throughout the day. It was June, and in the mornings beautiful sunlight streamed in, illuminating the whole space with the assistance of the halogen lights that shined like marbles; in the evening there was only artificial lighting. Some of the bulbs were rectangular and glowed, other smaller LEDs emitted a very pure white light. They were all switched on whenever there was an emergency, which wasn't an unusual occurrence. At night the lighting was left very low to encourage tranquility and sleep.

I was obsessed with the colors. White and green were the predominant hues, particularly the almost apple green of the nurses' and aides' uniforms. There were also blue uniforms, and face masks that slowly turned gray with use. Even the noise of the machines had a color. They sometimes started up without warning, and that frightened me.

My mood was constantly swinging. I still didn't know what had happened. How long had I been in that hospital? At times I felt like crying, but that was impossible. I'd gone for over twelve months without shedding tears, when normally anything would set me off.

One day a nurse handed me a strange piece of equipment with three round balls in a container with narrow compartments that connected to a mouthpiece. The young man said I had to blow hard to make the balls rise in their compartments. I didn't blow hard enough, I'd forgotten how. And anyway, I didn't understand why he wanted me to do it.

Early one morning I saw a dark liquid coming from the tube in my mouth. I was startled and signaled to one of the aides. I don't remember what explanation I was given.

The most beautiful sensation I had was when I saw my daughter arriving, calling, "Mom, they've taken it out!" She was radiant with joy and hope, her eyes were shining brightly and, even though I was still lying flat on my back, I understood that I would eventually leave that bed.

GUMS

It was July and the ice cream started melting the moment you left the Palazzo parlor; we'd been going there for months, like a ritual or religion that helped us hold out until nightfall when the heat dissipated in slender currents of air, and I'd have already had enough, and Ismael was pressing heart-shaped ice cubes wrapped in a T-shirt to his cheek. The ice cube tray had been a present from some-one at a wedding shower, which was only nominally so since Ismael and I still hadn't gotten married, but not long ago had decided to simulate a wedding so that, among other things, we could stop talking about weddings. He didn't want to get married and I did; I needed to explore the meanings of that act, cloak myself in a gesture; plus, I liked the idea of setting myself up in opposition to those proud parents of three who had never tied the knot or gone through the courts: I'd show them the photos of my sham wedding. So what do you think, Ismael? An album of joke photos? We've never celebrated anything. And at first it was a joke, like the Christmas cards we made with he and I as Joseph and Mary, wearing a couple of sheets and aluminum foil halos. López, our dog, was baby Jesus, his snout peeping out from the shawl I'd bought for my cousin Maite's graduation. The shawl was straw-colored; if I cut myself and López out from the rest of the photo, we'd be like that painting by Goya with a dog's head peeking over a slope. I felt bad about López, sorry to have made an animal look ridiculous. Did you and I look ridiculous dressed up as Mary and Joseph? Had our friends' smiles been embarrassed? I don't think so, but how can I be sure? I'd hoped to open a door with the sham wedding, enter an unknown room. I was itching for something that would turn everything on its head, longing to give birth to ravens instead of children. And I convinced myself that it would be a way of warding off bad luck. I didn't know how to explain it; and I didn't stop to analyze it either. I couldn't wait for February and our vacation to come around. We were able to get away that year because the exams would be done at Ismael's university and I was on a list of high school substitute teachers but hadn't had any work because of the cutbacks (cutbacks made me think of mulberry leaves being eaten by silkworms). The unemployment didn't bother me; my thing was cinema and I'd just won a prize in the *ONCE* lottery. I'd be living in the lap of luxury for the rest of the year and Ismael wouldn't have to find the rent alone.

My best friend had a house in the village of Robledondo, up in the mountains, about thirty miles from Madrid, and she offered it to us for the party. At the sham wedding shower there were no bee antenna headbands or penis tiaras; I just had some T-shirts printed with a photo of Ismael and I dressed as bride and groom. We toasted the Photoshop montage with white Rueda wine. I'd done a few trial runs using virtual suits and gowns, pasting our heads on like pinballs that fit any collar or neckline. At the very last minute I changed the venue of our vacation. We'd planned to spend the time in a friend's London home, but before I could buy the e-tickets, I saw an offer for three weeks in Lanzarote. Something gave way without any effort, and I went to the travel agency to put our names down; that evening I unfolded a map of the island on the table; almost everything was black: volcano craters like birds' nests and sparsely scattered towns. Ismael tensed; not that he was against the idea, it was more like a hunter that has spotted its prey in the distance. He said he'd always wanted to visit Lanzarote, but that you couldn't tell what color the island was from that map. We switched on the lamp and the ceiling light; neither offered us any further enlightenment. We didn't look on the internet either, preferring to live with the uncertainty of the map I'd been given at the travel agency, in which—according to Ismael—the island looked like an invertebrate. And we had things to sort out; there was a ton of Spanish omelet, sausage, and bowls of tabouli in the fridge, and we needed to take the seafood out of the freezer: the fishmonger had told us that the king prawns should be defrosted overnight. We also had to get to Robledondo early to organize the tables, but for me all that seemed a long way off, and I think the same was true for Ismael. In front of us, hanging from a set of coat hooks, were our costumes, which López was sniffing at that moment, his tail wagging. We'd decided that it would be best not to put them in the closet. As if we'd forget them! Even though my mind wasn't really on the wedding, I told Ismael that we could have gotten married for real; he responded that when that event occurred our friends would come to the party thinking it was a joke. The sham wedding suddenly seemed an absurdity, not at all what I'd intended; I suspected then that its only objective was to give me an excuse for something I'd been longing to do for ages: go to an island and gaze out over the ocean from the shore. I scrutinized the map again and it looked to me like a drawing of a leech. Ismael had been right to compare it to an invertebrate. I felt freed from my bones, plunged in ancient, placid forms of life.

We got up at seven and, after dropping López off at my parents' house, drove to Robledondo wearing jeans, our wedding clothes hanging from the straps above the rear windows and with a trunkload of food. I'd hardly slept all night, and dozed the whole way. Beatriz welcomed us with coffee, and we were in the garden before 10 a.m., hoping that the evening sun would later add an afterglow to the chalky clouds. It wasn't forecast to be cold; the winter had been warm, even in the sierra, and there were tables inside for those who felt the chill. By eleven, when we were dressing in silence, it was hot. Looking in the mirror, I felt a sudden, urgent need to go to the beauty salon to get my hair done: I'd never in my life been to a beauty salon. I asked Beatriz to be my stylist.

"How do you want it?"

"Whatever, but brush it for a while first. Will you do my makeup too?"

I closed my eyes and put myself in my friend's hands. The ceremony was very quick, the sun was warm enough to see us through the hours we were going to spend with the guests and the Ribeiro wine; I remember glancing across to a corner of the garden and seeing Ismael on all fours, eating grass, before I slipped away to the bathroom to throw up the pints of coffee and alcohol that had left me almost hysterically elated. But the wine had done nothing to diminish the feeling of senselessness; what Ismael and I were doing was like picking at scabs, but there at the party, slightly drunk, it was like we were the scabs. Despite what I say now about the drink and the brief shiver of cold whenever I stood still, we had a good time: me in my cream, retro twenties dress and the simple hairstyle that Beatriz created; Ismael in his suit and bow tie. "Haven't you told your parents?" I asked him. I knew he hadn't, and I hadn't said anything to mine either, just that we were going on vacation, but there were moments I regretted our lack of parental support. We'd probably end up hiding the photos of the sham celebration in the back of the closet, far from our children's eyes. We'd take them out when the kids grew into sophisticated humans. The party went on well into the night; the next day, at lunchtime, we boarded our flight to Lanzarote in a lamentable state. I had no memory of what I'd packed and neither did Ismael. We were too tired to sleep. As the plane approached the island we glued our faces to the window, me sitting on Ismael's lap, trying to recognize its black outline. The only color was the indigo of the ocean, which rose upward until it filled the air with a blue haze. We couldn't see volcanoes or anything else until we began to descend and were offered a clear image of the coastline; it must have been very windy because there was a lot of turbulence. Then, for a few seconds, it seemed like we'd stopped, that the aircraft was hanging motionless with the unruffled calm of a bird. It was just an impression; the plane landed. Everything returned to coal black and rays of light on a barren surface.

We spent the first four days between Playa Quemada and Timanfaya National Park, hopping barefoot over volcanic rocks. Our sham wedding began to make sense during those days, a different kind of sense that I couldn't quite put my finger on, but that gave me self-assurance. The hours melted over us as we sat on the beach with nothing around besides the gently sloping hillsides with their otherworldly palette of colors. Reds and blacks, and me determined not to spend any more time in front of the computer screen: that Martian desert was better than any virtual world. I used to get up in the mornings before Ismael to dive into the cold Atlantic and—let's be honest—to have a little time to myself; afterward I'd have breakfast in the bar in what was called the town, although it didn't seem like one to me. We never referred to it as such, but Playa Quemada was really a village. There were many other words that didn't pass our lips. We spent hours without formulating a single thought, swaddled in simple, infantile phrases: "I'm going for a swim. Bye." Or, once in the sea: "No one's ever going to drag me out of here." Ismael was reading up on the brain, and at night we talked about the ancient responses that contact with the natural world would produce in our bodies. We'd grow gills if we spent long enough consciously submerged in some remote underwater valley.

Ismael was as relaxed as me, as much at peace with the world, until one night, just when we were beginning to tan, the pain began, the same pain that a year before had forced him to cancel his classes to have flap surgery. On that occasion his whole mouth had become infected; he was shivering with fever as the dental surgeon removed a bespittled slice of gum. His moans in the night didn't stop me from getting up for my morning swim. I jumped out of bed the moment I opened my eyes, put on my bikini, and quietly left the room; I spent longer than usual in the water, foreseeing a morning of doctors and pharmacies, or just waiting around. Among the waves I was startled by the glint of a yellow fish. For a moment I did nothing, not quite believing my eyes, but also paralyzed with anger. I went to have breakfast, and instead of a tostada I ordered pickled anchovies. The man behind the counter told me that pickled anchovies weren't a house specialty, but he could do some limpets. I blushed and ordered a tostada with olive oil, a glass of juice, and a coffee; when I returned to our room, I wasn't surprised by what I found: an unwashed Ismael standing in front of the mirror, large pearls of sweat on his temples, the agony creasing his face, his whole body. The bathroom light fell with a diffused verticality, forming shadows and patches of light on his skin: he looked like a lizard. I stared at him coldly. He was absorbed in his new circumstances, and even though

I never asked, I know he hadn't noticed that I'd been gone an hour longer than usual. He seemed both horrified and ecstatic.

We managed to get an appointment with a dentist in Arrecife. Ismael was running a temperature and in the waiting room he had to clench his jaw to control the shivering. The dentist warned him that if he lanced the gum our vacation would be ruined. The best option would be to take antibiotics and go under the knife back in Madrid. Ismael still had lots of personal leave left; it would be no big deal if he took one or two more days. "The worst of it is the halitosis, but we can get by without kissing," he said when we'd left the dentist's office; I nodded just to make some response to that unabashed absurdity, as if our breath didn't always smell in the mornings. Perhaps what was embarrassing him was the disruption in the harmony of our bodies: all that rolling around on the rocks, fucking, feeling like eighteen-year-olds in the full flush of youth when I was well past thirty and he was forty. The antibiotics brought his temperature down, but he still didn't feel up to taking his sluggish jogs. In the following days he put on a brave face, and what he took to the beach was not the book about the brain, but his Kindle with his students' doctoral theses. He bought a newspaper and, between writing notes on the theses, glanced at it like a devoted reader. Newspapers were chill-out in material form. It was only on Sundays or when we were on vacation that Ismael allowed himself the luxury of spending the whole morning reading both the opinion columns and news, without the need to comment or pontificate on anything, accompanied first by a cortado and then a small beer when he got to the inserts two hours later, usually at Plaza de las Comendadoras if the weather was good, or in Le Pain Quotidien in winter, ordering an americano because he liked to dunk his buttered roll in the bigger cup. During the work week, reading was an obligatory action, especially now that the university was going down the drain and he was still only an associate lecturer, with years of anxious waiting ahead of him before he could expect to get tenure. It was enough to put anyone's nose out of joint. Despite having a PhD, I'd decided to retreat from university life before it was too late. I took my first steps into the world of cinema and one of my shorts won a prize in the Seville International Film Festival in the New Wave section. Ismael was unenthusiastic about the prize, and one night confessed that he didn't like my short. But whatever…the thing was that he felt he had to punish himself for the state of his mouth, so he turned to the theses—his original plan had been to read them on our return from Lanzarote—and I was left prowling around his towel, his beach hat, his childish figure: prowls that were actually escapes into the water since I had no desire to look at the Kindle loaded with theses; I didn't want them to be there but, at the same time, was grateful for them because—to be honest—I didn't want Ismael in the waves with me either, surrounding the experience with his sick ritual, his gaze fixed on mile after mile of light and haze. We'd rented a car to make a few excursions and I had no intention of changing that plan, to spend the days taking naps that did nothing for my digestion. Given the state of his health, there was nothing to stop him from sleeping the hours away. I missed him a little when, on the third day after his gum had given up the battle, I got into the car to drive alone to Timanfaya, but the next day I wanted to watch him be in pain, nodding off or prodding his cheek, washing his mouth out with Oraldene without ever getting rid of the bad smell. He got edgy if I came too close; true, a little morning breath was nothing compared to the stink of the decomposing food in his gum. The antibiotics hadn't restored the membrane to its proper state. In fact, the abscess had grown, and by then resembled a visor hanging over his tooth, around which were the visible remains of rotting food that Ismael removed with a Q-tip soaked in antiseptic. He never managed to clean it thoroughly, the swelling remained red. The dentist had told him not to poke at it, but he was convinced that his efforts could only improve the ulcerous appearance of his gum. But the fact was that all his poking around just made the stink worse. While I was driving to Timanfaya, I pictured his neurotic behavior. Ismael wasn't going to count the hours I was absent because he would be using them to wash his mouth out with Oraldene and search the internet for worst case scenarios—an endless chain of stories about gums destroyed by tumors—rather than solutions to his problem. And exactly why had his gum swelled? Isn't that a pretty weird occurrence only a medical doctor can discuss convincingly?

In the evenings we continued walking to Arrecife for dinner; Ismael always ordered limpets, which were served in a black pan, and were like eyes dully gleaming in a room with the shutters closed. I'd pop one of those formerly untasted mollusks into my mouth as if expecting to encounter signs of life. In the meantime, he'd be trying unsuccessfully to disguise an eagerness that reached its peak as I held the creature between my teeth, and when I finally swallowed it, he'd attack his food with gusto. I'd then tuck into my fresh bream with equal gluttony, and neither of us would raise our eyes until our plates were clean. We couldn't bear each other in those moments. But the tension only lasted as long as it took us to empty a bottle of wine (Ismael was ignoring the contraindications for the antibiotics), and then we either had gin and tonics at the bar on the esplanade or in the hotel, looking out over the dark sand. Google Earth showed ninety-nine houses in Playa Quemada. I got the urge to explore the town by night, when the streets were like empty highways. There was nothing to stop me from leaving Ismael on the terrace, with his gin and his ruminations about his foul smelling abscess. I felt uncomfortable around him, and when guilt about my lack of sympathy kicked in, I'd tell him I was glad we'd celebrated our sham wedding. I wasn't lying. I've never lied to him. Nevertheless, on one of those nights, when he was idly stirring his gin and tonic in the shadows of the terrace, it occurred to me that it would make no difference if, instead of staying, I headed out into the streets, and that's just what I did, being careful to close the door quietly so he'd think I was in the room, checking my email. Once outside, I was unable to go any farther. I stopped for an egotistical reason: getting into an argument with Ismael would mean the end of my idleness. I returned to the room; he was lying on the bed and simply said:

"I didn't hear you say you were going out."

"That's because I didn't."

The following day I took the car before Ismael had time to notice. The fleshy visor covering putrefying food didn't stop him from eating a breakfast of toast and all the sausage at the buffet, then polishing off a lunch of garlic potatoes with a pan of limpets. I'd think about leeches as I watched him chew the tough flesh of mollusks that were so unappreciated on the mainland, and which, when raw, looked just like Ismael's infected gum. I drove to Timanfaya to walk barefoot; there were hardly any tourists there at that time in the afternoon. I sat at the base of a small crater; afterward, I walked for an hour without losing sight of the car, which I'd pulled off the road for fear of a police car passing. Although, to be honest, I'd yet to see a single police officer. Neither my urban nor rural senses worked in Timanfaya, so I didn't know where to focus my worries. Some of the volcanoes formed rock corridors; in addition to fossilized plants, I found the remains of things that had once lived in the ocean. When the sun began to go down, I sat on the hard sand. Then I saw them.

After ten days of watching Ismael dip those slimy marine creatures into green sauce there was absolutely no doubt. Perhaps if I hadn't found them repulsive, I'd have mistaken them for mussel shells, or fossils that hadn't been engulfed by lava, because they only just showed above the gray and strangely iridescent tegument of a terrain that— and I swear this is true—at midday looked like the sea. I was lying flat on my stomach to hear the silence of the dry lava, the peacefulness of the cones, the dead calm that made me think of imminent eruptions. I started scraping at the earth with my fingertips and pieces of rock; what I found were the remains of limpets, as if all the restaurants and hotels tipped the shells in the park. The sea was too far away to account for their presence. Rather than marine dwellings or pieces of beach-themed jewelry, I've always thought of shells as skeletons. The souvenir stores at seafronts, with their tellina and conch shells, seemed more to me like bone traders. When I put one of those miniature crypts to my ear I don't hear the sound of the sea, but the spirit of the mollusk, its sticky soul slithering over the nacre.

Although on a small island you're never very far from the coast, twenty kilometers was too far. I wasn't frightened by the presence of those carcasses; what terrified me was that the limpet shell might have penetrated Ismael's gum. It made no sense: the infection, the dentist had assured us, had to do with the growth of the flesh. According to him, the body tends to fill cavities, but sometimes fails in that endeavor. I picked up a shell and put it to my nose; at first I could only smell volcanoes, their rocky bodies. Then I perceived the foul smell of Ismael's mouth, of my non-husband's gum, but I put it down to my olfactory imagination or tiredness. As the subtle smell became a source of pestilence, it forced me to turn around, thinking that Ismael was behind me. For me, ghosts are never the spirits of strangers. They are the people I love most dearly. I threw the shell far away and on my next outing avoided any communion with the silent earth. Instead, I took Highway 704 to an unnamed turn-off that led to the coastal zone of

Timanfaya Park. There was no silence since the waves were breaking against the black cliffs; I went down to the beach and spent the afternoon there, surrounded by pebbles and every imaginable form of shell, including limpets. The Atlantic smelled of stagnant seaweed, and I clung to that rank smell as a sort of explanation for what had happened. I clung to it without conviction, as a predictable line of argument; it was clear that the smell of the seaweed was as mild as that of the sea anemones on the coast of Cádiz, while Ismael's mouth made you think of bile.

That night my non-husband greeted me with shining eyes that skittered around in the darkness. The windows were closed, as if Ismael was protecting the room from the exterior sunniness, or more like: as if he wanted to shield his new smell. Outside, the air had already cooled, which accentuated the embarrassing stink of his mouth.

"Why have you closed all the windows?"

He smiled at me over the screen of his laptop. His eyes reminded me of crickets.

"Sorry, I hadn't realized," he said.

I threw the windows wide open, including the one in the bathroom, as if I wanted the violence of the action to wrench them from their frames. Ismael didn't turn a hair; he was focused on his internet search. I took a shower and then, instead of going to Arrecife, we stayed in the hotel. The out-of-season watermelon was the only thing at the buffet that appealed to me and, when we returned to our room, his eyes still had that insect appearance. He came up close and French kissed me, the first kiss since his mouth had started to bother him; he was unembarrassed about passing his breath or saliva to me, so I leaned back to move my mouth down to his neck and other sweeter smelling parts of his body. Ismael, however, gently licked my face and again put his mouth before mine. He began some strange form of smooching that consisted of sucking in his cheeks to stimulate his salivary glands and transfering the putrid liquid to my mouth, making me salivate too. After two or three bouts of retching, the spasms began to ease, as did my tears. I wasn't crying from emotion; those tears were caused by the contractions of my diaphragm. The spasms made my face turn red; I was suffocating.

"If I stop, it will only get worse," he whispered with strange, pensive tenderness; his serenity was like that in a church after a service.

He put his lips back onto mine. I swallowed disgusting spittle, and didn't have the impression of being kissed; it was as if I were performing oral sex because the other person couldn't copulate in any other way. When it was over Ismael went to the bathroom to clean his gum with his usual thoroughness, which in some way made me feel more relaxed. He got into bed after chewing two sticks of chlorophyll gum, and his kiss was dry, tight-lipped, carefully preventing any leakage. I was about to suggest that we take an early flight home; even though his temperature was normal, his gum showed no signs of improvement. Then I thought of the time remaining and saw myself not with Ismael, but walking in Timanfaya. I didn't speculate about what we'd just done. It was like a siesta with nightmares you can't draw any conclusions about because you've forgotten their content. You just float on the sensation, and that's what I was doing, floating while enjoying my last days in Lanzarote.

The next afternoon, I didn't go to Timanfaya. I had no desire to see the shells again, but knew that the instant I set foot in the park I'd be hooked and would start scratching the earth in search of them. I was sorry not to be able to walk tranquilly among the volcanoes. My lungs seemed to expand in that terrain, and I felt that such an organic communion with the earth was now going to be necessary if I wanted to keep on breathing. In La Geria, on the edge of the park, I had a glass of red wine and then walked, under the watchful eyes of the waitress, between the walls like wrought iron where the grapevines grow, which, together with the ash used as fertilizer, formed a picture that was clearer than the land, with its green-leafed stumps. When I remembered that I hadn't brought any provisions along, I bought a bottle of wine. From La Geria, I drove to Asomada and wandered for a while in the unseasonably strong sun among intensely white houses that I coveted. The sheer din of the light, its vitality, sounded pleasurably in my nervous system; although the fact was that life there must be melancholy, which is what I liked about the place. I consulted my guidebook and chose a more urban environment as my next stop: San Bartolomé, where I spent the rest of the afternoon watching locals dressed in traditional costumes carry their patron saint from one shrine to the next. I was the only tourist. I returned to the hotel after nightfall and, in the darkness, couldn't tell if Ismael's eyes were looking like insects. When I took the small bottles of liquor from the fridge they immediately misted over.

In San Bartolomé I'd stocked up on a variety of cold cuts.

"We're having dinner here," I said.

We ate and sipped the La Geria wine sitting on the bed; the windows were open and the TV off. It was hot, the air in the room smelled of the decay in Ismael's mouth, and we hadn't switched on the television because we wouldn't have known what to watch. Ismael talked about his plans for a real wedding ceremony. He said "wedding ceremony" but I decided that he meant that he was dreading surgery, thinking back with distaste on our sham wedding. It wasn't its falseness that unsettled me but the fact that it seemed to have taken place in some distant era, or even never at all. The gum was the only real thing, and Ismael's plans sounded like detailed advice on dental hygiene taken from the internet in an attempt to discover how to destroy the food debris trapped there. "But there's something else I've got to tell you," he added, barely giving me time to ask "what" before continuing: "I'm turning into an insect." I cracked up and Ismael also laughed, but without ceasing to talk. "It's not just flesh covering my tooth. Honestly." He sat down near the bedside lamp and said, "Look." I practically had to put the lamp into his mouth as his cheeks cast a shadow: it was true, what lay under the visor was not simply the miserable tooth, dotted with the particles of food Ismael was constantly trying to remove. There was also another sort of tissue, reminiscent of the tight-fitting shell of a beetle. I held my breath; the smell seemed especially bad that day, passing to my taste buds as if the sensation entered through my tongue rather than my nose. My retching had been conquered by the experience of the night before.

"It must be crystallized foodstuffs," I commented with complete sincerity, as if I'd spent my whole life using a term I'd just invented. What are "crystallized foodstuffs"?

He was frightened, not because he believed that he was turning into an insect, but by my lack of surprise at his declaration. We gazed at each other and I became aware that we were experiencing the same sense of fear. Ismael said:

"Best not to overthink it."

I had the urge to reply that there was nothing to over-think and no Wikipedia page or website was going to an-swer our questions, no matter how long he spent surfing the internet trying to scrape together knowledge about pu-trifying flesh. The hypothesis that he was turning into an insect was most likely the result of hours of research in the virtual world. Ismael never did things by halves.

"What's important to me now is a proper marriage," he pronounced, and this time there was no way I could misinterpret that as any dread of surgery.

"But you didn't dread the surgery the last time you had a problem with your gum," I persisted. "And ice cream helped. Don't you remember? Cold things stop the inflam-mation. The dentist said that too."

"I'm not talking about that," he replied.

I didn't insist. He moved away from the lamp. Although we'd already had our dessert and were making Cuba Libres with the bottles from the minibar, he took a plastic container from the fridge. Ismael's movements had lost that touch of indecisiveness, that characteristic mo-ment of hesitation so indicative of his pensive nature. The way he moved to the fridge was as nimble as a cockroach scuttling away when it feels itself cornered. The container held cold limpets in sauce.

"Where did you get that?" I asked.

"It's the leftovers from lunch."

"I'm going to take a walk," I said before he could choose one of the limpets and put it in his mouth, and once I was outside I realized that I was abandoning him there with his wedding plans.

The streets had a rundown air. I walked barefoot on the asphalt for some indefinite time, taking no notice of its roughness on my soles. The bar where I usually had breakfast was open. A huge TV screen I'd never noticed in the mornings was showing a Steven Seagal movie with the volume on high. The waiter greeted me and I couldn't help feeling slightly uneasy. I hadn't expected him to recognize me. In the mornings, after my swim, I always turned up wearing sunglasses, a sarong, and with my hair tied back; if he knew it was me, then there wasn't much difference between making an effort to look good and walking straight out of the water with your face all salty and your hair a mess. I sat down with a vivid consciousness of the pointlessness of making plans: there were limpets in the chill case, and though I was ready for my third drink of the night, that fleshy mollusk whetted my appetite. I hadn't slept well or eaten properly for days and was only just becoming aware of that fact; and it wasn't Ismael's fault that we'd stayed at the hotel instead of going to Arrecife.

"I'd like some limpets," I told the waiter.

"They are delicious," he replied.

He took the tray of raw sea creatures from the chill case and disappeared into the kitchen. While he was preparing the limpets, I ignored the calm sea and counted the wintry-looking flies lying around the display unit instead; those flies must be frozen, just like Ismael, or rather: Ismael was capable of freezing at a temperature that kept the limpets free of bacteria, although there was nothing to indicate that the flies were frozen rather than simply dead. In the latter case, their perfect stillness could be explained by the grime stuck to the surface of the glass. The flies had settled there and had then been unable to unstick themselves. I ate my dish of limpets without feeling nauseated by their connection to the flies' bodies or Ismael's illness and I left the bar with a holder of strawberry and vanilla ice cream cones, my non-husband's favorite flavors; I ran back to the hotel terribly afraid that the ice cream was going to melt, and when Ismael saw what I was carrying he asked why I'd paid for them when ice cream was available for free from the buffet.

"Try one," I said, ignoring his observation. Then I made sure that he bit into the ice cream using the side of his mouth nearest the decaying flesh; the tension between us eased as the stink mingled with the sweet scents of vanilla and strawberry; neither Ismael nor I asked ourselves why the extra-strength mints, the chlorophyll strips for bad breath, and all those other oral remedies didn't have the same effect.

After a while I asked him to show me the inside of his mouth. The strange shell was covered in unmelted ice cream that refused to mix with his saliva and looked like the flies in the chill case: it had some trick for retaining its composition during the process of decomposition. I felt triumphant, and believe Ismael did too, despite the fact that he couldn't spend all his time eating scoops of ice cream and that the effects were short lived. The next day, after lunch followed by a tub of chocolate and hazelnut ice cream, I plucked up the courage to return to Timanfaya and bury my hands in the sand in search of the shells; the weather was warmer than it had been on previous days, the earth looked closed in on itself, everything seemed tinged with nostalgia, and there was nothing where the shells should have been except for the pile of sand I'd dug up. I lay down on it, put my ear to the ground and, for the first time, thought seriously about Ismael's wedding plans, about attracting a more real form of bad luck. I allowed the calm to wash over me.

THE FORTUNE-TELLER

You've appeared in a client's tarot reading. I don't understand. Call me: 415-295-5143

While having breakfast at a Viena Capellanes she wondered if the person who had visited the clairvoyant was the man now sitting across from her, alternating sips of juice and latte as if attempting to create some specific effect on his taste buds or perhaps his health. In fact, she wasn't wondering that, just projecting the message from the clairvoyant onto the first person she saw. And that person turned out to be a man who had looked at her several times, and not distractedly. His attention might have been due to the fact that she'd also noticed him, and both of them had been attempting to draw conclusions about those glances. Something more had to happen to bring the situation to some form of closure; for example, he could come over to her table and say, "I went to a fortune-teller and she told me that I was going to meet someone while I was having breakfast." The man got to his feet. He'd left a few drops of juice in his glass. He paid at the counter and walked out onto Calle Fuencarral.

I'm seeing a short trip that will clarify many things.
Let's take a look. Call me: 415-295-5143

She got into the car and drove out of Madrid. Maybe
that's how it was. Not only refusing to take seriously
messages that were probably machine-generated (Could
anyone of her background, a middle-class woman down
on her luck, actually doubt that?). Not only refusing to
take them seriously, but also recognizing that any trace of
superstition would open up a crack to a possibility that,
in her case, was as remote as the existence of God. And
that crack was equivalent to relinquishinng her sense of
pride. If she put it down to imagination or desire, the crack
could be as wide as she wanted, wide enough to generate something like, for example, the fact that she is now
on the road, has passed El Escorial heading for Zarzalejo,
and is taking her foot off the gas pedal because a dense
fog has fallen on the foothills, limiting visibility on whole
stretches of the highway. It had been a long time since
she'd taken the car out with no other objective than to
drive. In the past she'd done that with partners, and it was
always better when they did the driving because when she
wanted to let her thoughts roam free she preferred not to
have to keep her eyes on the road. Setting out on a "short
trip" that would "clarify many things." Was her excursion
a short trip? How far would she have to go and how long
would she have to remain wherever she ended up for her
wandering to constitute a short trip? And what exactly
needed to be clarified? She sat near a heater in a bar in
Zarzalejo, a notebook, pen, and cup of decaffeinated coffee

on the table in front of her. Of course she needed to clarify many things in her life, but none of them required the urgency suggested by the clairvoyant's message. That message alluded to problems whose resolution couldn't be put off. For example, deciding to set up an editorial services company of her own. However, the problems she listed in her notebook weren't of that nature; they were more long-term, vague, related to the sorts of on-going debates in which someone, perhaps she herself, would claim that it was the way things were, or a simple matter of inertia. An image came to mind: her childhood living room in semi-darkness, a television set that had been left on for hours, violent, narcotic tedium. Two people fading away in front of the screen. Then on Monday morning, after a weekend of exasperating nothingness, those two people went to work, returning with fresh air and other preoccupations that pulled them far back from the edge of the abyss and made the two hours from ten to midnight on the couch in front of the television a simple period of rest, a break before facing the world again. Some weekends they avoided the couch and got in the Volkswagen Passat to travel through other provinces, and that was a pleasant form of getting away from it all, spending time observing other realities. She, their daughter, would be in the back seat with her Walkman. Also in a world of her own.

It was still a mystery to her why a computer that sent random messages had a telephone number.

And what would have happened if she'd gone over to that man's table and handed him a scrap of paper with her email?

Whenever I do your tarot I get a conflict between
three people. One of them is going to back down. Call
me: 415-295-5143

Zoe's name didn't fit her. When I first saw her I thought
she should dye her hair some color that suited her better:
that dirty, dark, ash-blond was even worse than the over-
the-top variety—like a light bulb or a highlighter pen—
that only looks good on a small number of women. Her
face had a moisturizer sheen; her clothes ran the whole
range of shades between brown and beige. Everything
about her was on that spectrum. She read romantic fiction, corrected proofs, and her name didn't fit her. Zoe sat
across from her in the office where she'd accepted a shit
awful job. Chances to publish her writing had been thin
for six months, and a friend had told her that he was leaving a temp job that consisted of inputting a catalogue into
Excel. She detested Excel but for working only two hours
a day, Tuesday to Thursday, she earned three hundred euros a month. Twelve euros fifty an hour for that shit awful
work. Lots of people had told her it wasn't so bad, that the
pay could have been worse, but for her the job was as bad
as they came. Zoe's desk was across from the computer
with the Excel sheet she had to fill in without getting the
lines mixed up or missing works from a catalogue that was
fifty percent self-published books, with the other half being grant-assisted. Most of them were written by men who
were either local celebrities or former academics over the
age of seventy; for example, a book called *Twilight of the
Aged Olive Tree* was by a writer from Jaén called Bernabé

Gómez, born in 1937, who was a professor at the Jaén Institute. The book was funded by the Torredonjimeno City Council.

Zoe was the proofreader who knew the most about everything. She could rattle off whole passages of Manuel Seco's works on lexicography and the *Diccionario panhispánico de dudas*. On her right was the second proofreader, María Isabel, an overweight brunette whose wardrobe generated images of Sunday mornings in some parish church in the Estrella neighborhood. She also read romantic fiction. The two women spent their working days correcting the galleys of books by retired philosophy professors of the Complutense or Autónima universities or poets who wrote about depression and nostalgia under the holm oaks of their native soils. On their journey home on the metro they read their romantic novels. Zoe was spectacularly good at catching mistakes. "If I have time before going to bed," she'd say, "I write to the publishers to point out the errors." María Isabel was slow and clumsy, and wore a permanently offended expression. She was the one who found cause for complaint about the new Excel-sheet filler. "The boy that was here before you was such fun," she said one day. "He used to tell us stories about his girlfriends and we'd give him advice." She smiled politely. The message was that Zoe and María Isabel found her boring: she never told them anything. She entered the office in silence and left without offering more than answers to work-related questions. Her opinion of the proofreaders must have shown on her face and in her habit of avoiding contact. Things were different with the office manager.

She was the only employee to have a golden parachute; she didn't read romantic fiction, probably didn't read anything else either. She was tall, with short hair and a seductive, slightly masculine voice, and she dressed like a nun. Sometimes she was tempted to ask the office manager if she belonged to the Teresian Association, but was afraid of offending her. Her name was Paz, and she wasn't annoyed when María Isabel denounced her. "Denounced" is probably a slight exaggeration: "ratted her out" would be better. María Isabel had told Paz that she was putting down three hundred euros on her monthly time sheets. "That new girl is taking us for a ride," she could imagine María Isabel having said to Paz and the boss before she arrived at the office. When she switched on her computer, María Isabel came over to her table and said:

"Your time sheets are wrong. You've been writing down three hundred euros a month when your pay is only two hundred. That's more per hour than I earn."

She hadn't been aware that her pay was only two hundred. She must have misunderstood, she said, and she wasn't lying. For María Isabel, the very idea of a temp earning more per hour than her seemed a conclusive, irrefutable argument, especially when she didn't take into account that temps had to pay their own social security. She herself had done the math and worked out that if that shit awful job were a person's only source of income, they wouldn't have even been able to afford those payments. But she still felt guilty. María Isabel now had a justification for her permanently offended expression, and even Zoe looked at her askance. They both preferred to side with the hated, exploitative boss rather than a misfit. Only Paz kept her thoughts to herself: if she had a poor opinion of her, she didn't let it show. Or maybe she just couldn't have cared less.

She'd held out for a few more weeks and then said she was leaving. Her last paycheck was a hundred euros.

"Whenever I do your tarot I get a conflict between three people. One of them is going to back down."

She'd been the one to back down.

She could consider other problems, but none of them fit so cleanly.

Petty bouts of jealousy between cousins.

Suspected minor betrayals: a friend who'd told a third party something she'd confided to him, showing that he was incapable of keeping secrets.

She and her parents escaping from the semi-darkness of the living room.

Was she doing the same thing with the clairvoyant's message as when she slipped that short trip into her life-line, but in some more subtle way, giving a new meaning to her memories?

Crying bitter tears for you, I see it night and day. I
know you don't believe me. Call: 415-295-5143

She didn't bother to try to work out which of her former partners was crying his eyes out for her. On this occasion too, it was more tempting to generate the situation, although she wasn't going to do it with any man. She visited her aunt and asked for the keys to the house that had belonged to her grandmother, who'd died just two months before. She bought a golden retriever puppy, put it in the car, and drove to her hometown. The puppy rode in the passenger seat, wagging its tail happily and licking her hand every time she changed gear. When she reached the family home she filled a large dish with water and another with dog food and put them in the master bedroom. Then she carried the puppy up to that old room, still smelling of salt and fat, where her grandmother used to cure hams. She locked the puppy inside for a day. The dog's constant whines prevented her from getting any rest. To escape the noise, she took a drive through the valley, walked for two hours through a holm-oak wood, and climbed to a ruined castle. She stopped at three bars along the highway. That night she played albums by groups she hadn't listened to since her teenage years with the volume up: Slayer, Cradle of Filth, Black Sabbath, Theatre of Tragedy. From time to time she paused the music to listen to the puppy's howls. It was a Tuesday in February; the family home occupied a whole block, and her only concern was that the puppy's howling could be heard from the street. But none of the neighbors appeared to have contacted her aunt and uncle to tell them about the noise coming from the house. The bedroom was well soundproofed. At four in the morning, when the whining had quieted, she considered the possibility that the puppy was dead. She drank more beer and didn't turn down the music until the sun was high in the sky. When she went up the stairs to the bedroom she was too drunk to feel fear. She opened the door; the puppy ran to her. Despite its obvious weakness, it continued wagging its tail. Maybe it was only confusion. It had vomited and was shivering.

> Miracles and clairvoyance are real. But there are a lot
> of sly dogs around. I suggest a Hidden Truth Tarot.
> Call: 415-295-5143

She was surprised that the last message should be a mere comment on fortune-telling. She'd never at any time expected anything from those messages. Yet they did seem weirdly appropriate, not only because they could be adapted to her situation or lead her to create new situations, but because they manifested their own shadow. And that shadow reminded her of her own. It was like the photograph of a highway on the outskirts of the city, at night, in a storm. Her childhood fears were there. When she was a little girl she used to kneel on the seat of the car and look out the back window at the falling rain. When the wipers swept away the drops there would be an instant when the outlines of the vehicles behind were sharply defined, before they were blurred again by the rain. It was in that blur stretching back into darkness, bordered by lights, that her fear was precisely located, and she couldn't take her eyes off it. Children didn't have to wear seatbelts in those days and the distances always seemed greater because the roads had only two lanes and were full of potholes. But it could be said that the messages from the clairvoyant that appeared regularly on her cellphone were a manifestation of her own shadow. And the last message fit perfectly with something she'd been thinking through for months. Once she'd rid herself of any trace of faith and even the desire to go on playing the game, she *miraculously* received a message that was like the final promise of an unfaithful lover. I'll never do it again. Miracles happen and clairvoyance exists.

ACKNOWLEDGMENTS

I would like to thank Rubén Bastida, María Lynch, Recaredo Veredas, and Alberto Olmos for their close readings and suggestions. Also the Residencia de Artistas Roquissar for its time.

The story "Rabbit Island" is dedicated to Sancho Arnal, a true inventor.

ELVIRA NAVARRO won the Community of Madrid's Young Writers Award in 2004. Her first book, *La ciudad en invierno* (The city in winter), published in 2007, was well received by the critics, and her second, *La ciudad feliz* (*The Happy City*, Hispabooks, 2013), was given the twenty-fifth Jaén Fiction Award and the fourth Tormenta Award for best new author, as well as being selected as one of the books of the year by *Culturas*, the arts and culture supplement of the Spanish newspaper *Público*. *Granta* magazine also named her one of their top twenty-two Spanish writers under the age of thirty-five. She contributes to cultural magazines such as *El Mundo* newspaper's *El Cultural*, to *Ínsula*, *Letras Libres*, *Quimera*, *Turia*, and *Calle 20*, and to the newspapers *Público* and *El País*. She writes literary reviews for *Qué Leer* and contributions for the blog *La tormenta en un vaso*. She also teaches creative writing.

CHRISTINA MacSWEENEY received the 2016 Valle Inclán prize for her translation of Valeria Luiselli's *The Story of My Teeth*, and *Among Strange Victims* (Daniel Saldaña París) was a finalist for the 2017 Best Translated Book Award. Among the other authors she has translated are: Elvira Navarro (*A Working Woman*), Verónica Gerber Bicecci (*Empty Set; Palabras migrantes/Migrant Words*), and Julián Herbert (*Tomb Song; The House of the Pain of Others*). She is currently working on a second novel by Daniel Saldaña París, and her translations of a short story collection by Julián Herbert were published in 2020.